LOVE'S WAITING GAME

Glenna Finley

Man is the hunter; woman is his game:
The sleek and shining creatures of the chase.
*—*TENNYSON

A SIGNET BOOK

NEW AMERICAN LIBRARY

Publisher's Note

PUBLISHER'S NOTE

NAL BOOKS ARE AVAILABLE AT QUANTITY DISCOUNTS WHEN USED TO PROMOTE PRODUCTS OR SERVICES. FOR INFORMATION PLEASE WRITE TO PREMIUM MARKETING DIVISION, NEW AMERICAN LIBRARY, 1633 BROADWAY NEW YORK, NEW YORK 10019

SIGNET TRADEMARK REG. U.S. PAT. OFF. AND FOREIGN COUNTRIES REGISTERED TRADEMARK—MARCA REGISTRADA HECHO EN CHICAGO, U.S.A.

SIGNET, SIGNET CLASSIC, MENTOR, PLUME, MERIDIAN AND NAL BOOKS are published by New American Library, 1633 Broadway, New York, New York 10019

First Printing, January, 1985

1 2 3 4 5 6 7 8 9

PRINTED IN THE UNITED STATES OF AMERICA

1

There was an ominous, considering look on Danielle Livingstone's face that was at odds with the rest of her appearance as she stared into the steaming thermal pool near Yellowstone's Old Faithful. It went unnoticed by most of the passersby who were surveying the attractions of the Upper Geyser Basin. Two young men, however, lingered hopefully at her elbow. Obviously they found a five-foot-four-inch blond who was attractively packaged in trim-fitting jeans of more interest than the other natural wonders. They took time to admire her pale honey-colored hair and classic profile and then tried to strike up a conversation. That stopped abruptly when Dany turned a freezing glance on them that would have lowered the temperature even in the thermal pool and showed that the Ice Age could return without warning.

Once Dany had the Crested Pool to herself again, she gave an exasperated sigh and went over to perch on the slatted bench at the edge of the wooden sidewalk. Normally she wouldn't have been so decidedly unfriendly even to strangers. She'd been in Yellowstone long enough to enjoy the atmosphere of informality and camaraderie among the visitors. Dany had felt that way herself—until she'd been stopped by the clerk at the front desk of the inn that morning. She was given a message marked "urgent" and directed to call her office at the first opportunity. Until that moment she'd blessed the old-fashioned facilities of the big hostelry which scorned such things as room phones and left guests pleasantly unencumbered by other modern touches like radios and television.

Dany hadn't missed them in the week she'd been staying at Old Faithful—she also hadn't missed her office at all. Or, more specifically, the president of Fremont Consultants—one Gregory Fremont, whose name was at the bottom of her telephone summons.

It was probably one of the few times in Greg Fremont's life that he'd ever been at the bottom of anything, she decided bitterly, and glared at the thermal pool in front of her, which was starting to burp with a vengeance in a new cycle. It was a damned shame that her so-called vacation had been subjected to a violent repercussion as well.

She'd held off returning the phone call while she ate breakfast—like a toothache sufferer sitting in a dentist's waiting room and hoping the pain will subside before the appointment comes due.

Like most fantasies, nothing happened in Dany's case to put off her return call; Old Faithful didn't inundate the inn with a steaming shower and there weren't any thunderstorms gathering on the horizon to knock out the phone lines.

Even after she dialed the Chicago number, she crossed her fingers and hoped that her employer would be unavailable. There was a little more chance for success in that daydream because Dany knew very well that the head of Fremont Consultants wasn't palpitating to hear from her either. He'd made that more than clear six months before when he'd come back from the West Coast division of the company to take control after his father had retired.

It wasn't a case of indulgent nepotism; Dany had heard all about Gregory Fremont's astute business tactics since she'd joined the company two years before. That was after she'd found that a college degree with a major in the classics wouldn't go far toward providing three meals a day. Fortunately, she'd been aware of this in college and had prudently taken a few commercial courses, as well. Those, coupled with some ongoing evening classes toward an advanced degree in business had established her on Fremont's top management floor, serving as executive secretary to Gregory Fremont's father. After his retirement, she hadn't wanted his son to feel that he'd inherited her along with the office furniture, so she'd requested a transfer to the legal section, where she settled in comfortably.

Unfortunately, it only took a morning for Greg Fremont to decide that he didn't like the substitute the personnel department had found for him. A little more questioning on his part revealed that Miss Livingstone could be reached at her new desk just down the corridor. Five minutes later, Dany had looked up from her typewriter when a six-foot specimen of annoyed masculinity slammed through her office door.

She was startled into hitting a wrong key at the intrusion and it wasn't any effort to match the man's scowl as he stood in front of her desk. "Most people knock," she told him, determined not to quail under his take-apart glance.

"I'll have to remember," he replied caustically.

She hesitated then before managing to ask, "Was there something you wanted?"

"Preferably a secretary who doesn't misspell words with more than two syllables. Is your name Livingstone?"

Her chin went up as she gave him the barest suggestion of a nod, and then she caught her breath sharply, remembering where she'd seen his chiseled features. The gray eyes had been just as piercing in a picture of the firm's board of directors in the annual report—only that view hadn't shown how his dark hair fell on his forehead when he raked it angrily as he was doing just then—nor had it shown how broad his shoulders were under a dark blue blazer. She had a very good glimpse of them as he put both hands on her desk and leaned toward her to say, "I'm Greg Fremont. What the devil do you mean by switching jobs? My father told me you were the best secretary he ever had."

"That was kind of him," she told him, keeping her words clipped and painfully polite. "I'm sorry if you've been put to any trouble. Actually I'm not sure how long I'll be staying with the firm, and it seemed better to make a switch now rather than inconvenience you later."

"I'm not keen on people who make up my mind for me." Greg stood upright again and shoved his hands in his pockets. "I've been making decisions for quite a while now."

Thirty-three years, Dany could have told him. She even knew the exact date, since she'd mailed a birthday present for his parents just the month before. It was an effort for her to refrain from mentioning it, but she managed a cool "I'm sure you have" that didn't give her feelings away.

Greg's dark eyes rose skeptically—showing that she hadn't been as successful at hiding her reactions as she'd imagined. He let his gaze wander over her tense figure, as if making a note of the trim-fitting black cashmere jacket. He paused longer at the flattering glen-plaid pleated skirt. Dany flushed as she realized the hem had ridden above her knees, and she pulled it determinedly down before meeting his glance again.

"Was there anything else?" she asked, as if her entire afternoon were booked and she didn't have a minute to spare.

"Quite a few things." The new head of the firm reached over calmly and pulled the paper from her typewriter, ignoring her startled gasp of protest.

"What do you think you're doing?" she burst out furiously as he put it down on the desk in front of her. "You come charging in here—interrupting things—Mr. Lord needs that letter out before five."

It wasn't true. The nice old gentleman in the legal department had merely said "whenever it's convenient" because he was still surprised at inheriting a secretary of Dany's talents without finagling.

"Jim Lord can get his letter out. I'll send Miss Snyder to take over here."

"But she's *your* secretary—"

"Not any longer." Fremont walked back to the doorway, pausing to say over his shoulder, "Hurry it up, will you? I can't waste any more time today."

He was gone before Dany could mention all her carefully worked-out reasons why she couldn't possibly work as his secretary. "Dammit all!" she said furiously to the closed door, and almost heaved a heavy crystal paperweight in that direction, until her common sense intervened. But that same common sense didn't stop her from hotfooting it after Gregory Fremont, her cheeks flushed with indignation.

She erupted into his office complex, threw an apologetic look in the direction of Miss Snyder as she went through to the inner office and closed the connecting door firmly behind her.

Greg looked up, his frown becoming pronounced when he saw that the intruder wasn't Miss Snyder, whom he'd summoned just seconds before.

Dany threw down the gauntlet before he could say anything scathing about *her* intrusion. "You can't go around ordering people to do things they don't want to do," she told him angrily as she advanced toward his desk. "I had a very good reason for changing jobs—"

"What was it?" he wanted to know.

"—and I don't intend to change my mind. No matter what you say about it," she went on, disregarding his interruption. "This was still a free country the last time I checked."

He fixed her with a level look that showed he'd come to the end of his patience and wasn't impressed by her rhetoric. "Why don't you stop acting like Little Nell and tell me why you've suddenly developed this aversion to being an executive secretary in this company? My father didn't have anything to do with this, did he?"

"Of course not." Her eyes still flashed but her voice was considerably calmer. "Your father was a perfect gentleman."

"And you're implying that I'm not? Since we met for the first time about three minutes ago, I'd hardly call it a rational decision. Did you get scared by office gossip or do you just feel safer working for a man old enough to be your father?"

"That's ridiculous!" she spluttered.

"Not any more than your flight down the hall—leaving me with that . . . that . . ." He waved an arm toward his outer office as he searched for a noun to describe Miss Snyder.

"Be quiet—for heaven's sake. She'll hear you," Dany hissed, sure that half the company could furnish a blow-by-blow account of their conversation by then.

"Now who's being ridiculous? Whatever her failings, the woman isn't the type who listens at keyholes," he said with masculine scorn. "Actually she's very pleasant, but charm doesn't help when you can't spell."

"There's always a dictionary . . ." Dany began, and then said hastily before he contradicted her logic, "I know, I know. First you have to know where to look. Well, there are lots of other secretaries on this floor—"

"But I don't have time to interview them. I'm due in St. Louis tomorrow and New Orleans the day after that. In the meantime, I need someone in charge of this office who knows the ropes. If it's a question of more salary—"

"That isn't the point. I told you—I'm not sure how much longer I'll be staying with the company," she said, wishing that her voice sounded firmer.

"Have you had a better offer?"

"No, it's not that. It's well . . . personal."

His direct gaze pinned her like a specimen on a microscope slide. "A man, I suppose. That's the trouble with women in business."

"It's nothing of the sort," she countered heatedly. "And your father had more sense than to make generalizations like that."

"My father lived in an era when sex differences were a matter of record—not a competition." He broke off as a buzzer sounded. "Damn. *Now* what?"

As he snatched up the receiver on his intercom and snapped, "Yes, Miss Snyder," Dany had a chance to relax and reflect that already Greg had changed the look of things in his office. There were neat piles of papers on the broad desk where his father had kept the top clean. The heavy velvet drapes were gone from the broad windows behind him, replaced with vertical blinds which allowed more light in the big room. Only two or three leather chairs were left to recall the traditional atmosphere which Fremont senior had fostered. Dany saw Greg frown in concentration with the receiver still held to his ear, and realized that already the pace of the company had accelerated under his direction. The man in front of her was like the breeze coming in the window, chilling but refreshing, too, as it dispersed the stuffy air.

For the first time, she wondered if she'd been too hasty in changing jobs.

He must have sensed her indecision as he put the receiver down, because he glanced up almost warily. "Where were we?"

"I was saying that I didn't know how long . . ." She swallowed the next word as he put up a palm like a traffic policeman, cutting her off.

"I'm not asking you to sign a fifteen-year contract, Miss . . . Miss . . . er . . ."

"Livingstone," Dany said dryly. So much for her fatal fascination! The man couldn't even remember her name. The only thing that apparently had made an impression was her typing speed, which was in that personnel file in front of him.

He looked down at it for a moment so she couldn't see if his gaffe had embarrassed him. It certainly didn't show in his voice. "Livingstone's quite a mouthful," he said, consulting the file. "So's Danielle. What did my father call you?"

"Miss Livingstone," she told him with satisfaction.

His eyes came up, the glance arctic again. "As I said, that was a different era. However, the important thing now is to get you back where you belong. I need your help, Miss Livingstone. At least for the first few weeks of this transition time. Can I count on you?"

Damn the man! He hadn't left her with a single excuse, and behind that bland expression on his rugged face, she was sure he knew it. "If you put it like that . . ." she began weakly, only to have him cut her off again as he stood up, showing that the interview was at an end.

"Good. As soon as you get things changed around—I'll tell you what I want you to take care of while I'm gone. I'm sure it will all work out splendidly, Miss . . ."

She glared at him as he paused.

Then he said smoothly, "Miss Livingstone."

As she turned and went out the door, she was sure that her new boss had hesitated that last time quite deliberately. He had won the first round hands down and she had the sinking feeling that it wouldn't be the last one.

After that, an armed neutrality existed between them. It took two weeks for Miss Snyder to start speaking to her again, but that annoyance was lost in the shuffle. Greg Fremont was a dynamo to work for and he remained stiffly polite in any encounters that didn't involve invoices, work projections, or the latest balance sheets. The first time he'd offered to buy her dinner after they'd worked late, she refused firmly without any explanations. Two days later, he invited her to a business lunch and she begged off, saying she'd already made other plans. There were no invitations after that, and Dany told herself that she was glad. She almost believed it until she started fielding phone calls from a sultry-voiced woman who clearly felt no such restraints regarding her employer. Along with her other duties, Dany was suddenly instructed to send flowers and procure dinner reservations for two. She jotted down his orders and got out of his office without showing any reaction but as she sat down at her desk again, she felt as if she'd just been kicked in the stomach.

There was no use kidding herself any longer. All the things she'd heard about Greg Fremont should have warned her—especially the office grapevine, which reported casualty figures on all the female employees who'd been smitten. And now, dammit, she got weak in the knees every time she was within three feet of the man, while he treated her with an absentminded air that made her blood boil.

The fact that she had a three-week vacation in the offing was the only thing that kept her from submitting her resignation then and there. That, and feminine pride, which made her reluctant to go creeping off after having lost the battle to a man who didn't even know he'd won it.

The first week of her vacation hadn't changed her feelings or presented any solution to her problems, so seeing Greg Fremont's name on the telephone message was a devastating blow.

She'd finally placed her return call when she couldn't find an excuse for avoiding it any longer. Miss Snyder answered the phone and her frosty tones showed that, whatever her limitations on spelling, she had an excellent memory for other things.

"I wondered when you'd return the call," she

told Dany. "So did Mr. Fremont. Actually I had no idea whether you could even be contacted, but he insisted."

"I wasn't lost," Dany replied dryly, wishing that she hadn't acceded to his last-minute request that she leave a copy of her itinerary. "What's the matter? Is there a contract missing or a list of specifications?"

"I would know about that. And since Mr. Fremont isn't even in town, I can't ask him."

"Isn't in town! I don't understand—"

"I merely do what I'm told around here," Miss Snyder replied in a martyr's tone that set Dany's teeth on edge. The woman's attitude would have tempted St. Peter to go over to the other side. Dany took a deep breath and tried to sound pleasant as she asked, "Well, then, we might as well forget it. Just tell him that I'm sorry I couldn't contact him." She crossed her fingers as she murmured the last sentence, since she felt like sending up Roman candles at the way things had turned out.

"You can tell him yourself when you see him at . . ." Miss Snyder hesitated for a moment, as if consulting her notes, and then resumed. "At Big Sky. He plans to be there tonight too, and he'll get in touch with you. You're to stay there until he does."

"Now, wait a minute—it's only an overnight stop on my schedule. . . ."

"Possibly. On your original itinerary." Miss

Snyder made no attempt to hide the satisfaction in her tone then. "Mr. Fremont had to revise his own so he could fit you in."

"You have to be kidding. . . ."

"I never joke on my employer's time. Unlike some people in this company . . ."

Dany cut the woman off before she could get sidetracked on what was evidently a favorite theme. "What I meant was—I have my vacation planned. No matter what Mr. Fremont has in mind, I can't chop and change just on a whim—"

"I suggest you tell *him* that," Miss Snyder said, cutting in just as ruthlessly. "Besides, meeting him at the Big Sky place isn't changing anything." She obviously was consulting her notes again. "You'd planned to be there tonight anyhow. Isn't that right?"

"Yes, but . . ."

"Well, then, I really don't see why you're so upset."

You wouldn't, Dany decided resentfully. And the damnable part was that she couldn't protest any more or Miss Snyder's imagination would start working overtime.

"Does he know where I'm staying at the resort?" she asked finally, trying to sound businesslike about the whole thing.

"I doubt it, since you didn't go into details on your itinerary."

And if I had a chance to do it again, I'd have forgotten to leave a schedule at all, Dany thought rebelliously. After all, it *was* supposed to be a vacation.

"If there's nothing else, I should get back to work." Miss Snyder's firm tones cut into Dany's meanderings. "Mr. Fremont left a great deal to be done—he said that things had certainly piled up."

"I'm sure that you'll handle it all admirably," Dany soothed, knowing that the poor woman really doted on holding down the job. Which made it all the more ridiculous that Greg Fremont was so stubborn about it. All Miss Snyder needed was a crash course in spelling to settle the problem.

"Well, I don't anticipate too many difficulties." Miss Snyder sounded complacent again. "You might mention it to Mr. Fremont when you see him tonight."

Dany started to say "*If* I see him" and then decided against it. A burst of bravado wouldn't prove anything. Instead, she murmured, "I certainly will," and grimaced after she hung up an instant later.

She decided there wasn't any use postponing her departure just because she wasn't looking forward to confronting Greg. Big Sky resort was one of her favorite places and she'd been fortunate in borrowing a friend's condominium for her overnight stay there. If she hadn't had to get to her old home during her vacation, she would have enjoyed spending the rest of her time at the ski resort tucked so beautifully in the Montana mountains. She frowned as she thought of Greg Fremont stopping over there—he wasn't the type to stray so far from city streets and expense-account lunches.

As she checked out of the big old-fashioned inn at Yellowstone, she took a last fond look at the peeled wood stair railings and mammoth fireplace with one of the inevitable foreign tour groups gathered in front of it. Outside, as she waited for the bellman to load her things into her car, she caught sight of a puppy tethered to a sleeping bag and backpack. Undoubtedly his master was inside having a late breakfast before setting off again on a park trail. Dany tried to visualize Greg doing such a thing and shook her head—probably he'd be uncomfortable even with the luxurious accommodations at Big Sky. It would serve him right if he had to spend a weekend at her family's resort in Hell's Canyon, where she was due later in the week. A few days with intermittent electricity and limited quantities of hot water could certainly have a salutary effect on the man!

Dany came back to reality when she heard the bellman slam her car trunk, and she thanked him as she handed him a tip, acknowledging that the weather looked "pretty good" for her drive north.

The Park road to the west entrance was crowded despite the lateness of the season, and she was forced to keep her attention on her driving. As she passed through some of the other thermal areas, the familiar hard-boiled-egg smell saturated the atmosphere but she was soon into a stretch of endless green hillsides on either side of the road, where only a few rock faces broke the monotony.

Once out of the park and across the Montana state line, she increased her speed as the traffic thinned and eventually became definitely sparse. She stopped once in a particularly pretty roadside view area to eat the sandwich she'd carried from Old Faithful and sip coffee from her thermos. The view in front of her was far more spectacular than what she'd seen earlier in the morning; the green waters of the Gallatin River meandered lazily up the canyon in front of her. It was shallow at that part and there were snow-white rivulets as the currents moved over the rocks which looked like giant stepping-stones. Overhead, the clouds were white—unlike their more threatening cousins to the south—and the sky was the bright blue of picture postcards and fairy tales. When combined with the rugged rock cliffs and thick forestation on adjacent hillsides, it was an awe-inspiring sight. Dany finished her sandwich and drank her last cup of coffee slowly, reluctant to leave such a gorgeous, tranquil place.

She pulled into Big Sky around four o'clock that afternoon and parked at the bottom of the stairs leading up to her friend's skiing condominium. The rest of the parking area was almost deserted, which wasn't surprising, considering the season. In late September the lodge and condominiums were generally occupied only by die-hards who liked mountain scenery whatever the weather. Dany carried her overnight bag up the stairs to the top-floor condominium, which overlooked a small lake down by the highway. She murmured with appreciation when she entered the compact apartment, made even more cheerful with the late-afternoon sun coming in the big front window. She pottered around unpacking in the bedroom and debated taking a shower in the adjoining bath. It would be just one more delay before facing the moment of truth—namely one Greg Fremont—who was probably even then in the lodge wondering what had happened to her.

Fifteen minutes later, when she'd walked across to the rustic lodge and asked for him at the desk, she discovered that he had at least discovered the swimming pool to help pass the time.

"It's right around the corner," the young reception clerk told her. "Mr. Fremont said that he was expecting his secretary." She let her glance wander over Dany's jeans and plaid shirt. "Or have I made a mistake?"

Evidently she'd been expecting gray flannel or a tailored tweed, Dany thought with amusement. "I didn't have time to change," she said solemnly. "I've been feeding the bears at Yellowstone."

"Oh, but you're not supposed to . . ." the girl retorted before she caught sight of the amusement lurking in Dany's features. "I fell into that one, didn't I?" she admitted then. "But today we're all a little paranoid on the subject of bears.

One was sighted down on the meadow this morning, and we're telling everybody to give that area a wide berth. We think she has some cubs close by."

"In that case, you have a right to be paranoid. Which meadow are you talking about?" Dany asked, wondering if she were going to meet an enraged mother bear when she walked back to the condominium.

"Down the road a bit—by the golf course," the clerk assured her. "You don't have to worry unless you'd planned a hike down to the falls tonight. We've already warned Mr. Fremont."

"You mean, he was hiking?" Dany made no attempt to hide the amazement in her voice.

The clerk stared back at her wide-eyed. "He said something about it earlier, but now he's decided to wait until tomorrow."

"I see." Dany really didn't, but it was hard to second-guess her employer at any time. Probably the best thing to do was stop stalling and get the meeting over with. After all, his schedule at the resort was his own affair, and she doubted if even a mother bear with cubs and a sore paw would change it.

She thanked the reception clerk and made her way around the sunken lobby with its attractive Indian rugs and big fireplace. As she paused in the deserted dining room to admire its cathedral ceiling, she heard voices from one corner where the bar was located, but she didn't bother to look for Greg there. There was still pale afternoon sunshine and she knew he'd be outdoors at the poolside if he had a choice.

When she opened the door of the pool's circular glass windbreak screen and saw his long figure stretched out comfortably on a canvas lounger, she took a deep apprehensive breath. An instant later she let it out in a hurry when she saw he was deep in conversation with an attractive brunette who was relaxing on a lounger just an arm's length away. Even at that distance, Dany noted that the brunette had a voluptuous figure shown to maximum advantage in a dark blue bikini. She raised up on an elbow as Dany approached, and her smile faded.

Dany tried not to wilt under the woman's obvious annoyance as her employer adjusted his sunglasses and sat up to face her.

"Miss Livingstone, I presume," he said finally, swinging his long tanned legs to the ground and getting to his feet. "I was about to send out a search party."

Dany wanted to tell him that it was an old joke and she wasn't amused—except the set line of his mouth showed that he wasn't amused either, so she'd better not try.

"I just got word this morning that you wanted to see me," she responded, shoving her hands in the pockets of her jeans so that he wouldn't know how nervous she was.

"Is this a friend of yours, Greg?" the brunette asked, her voice showing her disbelief.

"Miss Livingstone's my secretary," he replied, keeping his glance on Dany. "Danielle, this is Georgia Rowland. Mrs. Rowland has a condominium here at the resort."

Dany murmured something inconsequential, surprised that Greg had used her first name in his introduction—something that hadn't happened since the first day she'd met him. Perhaps he wanted to give the brunette a false idea of their relationship—not that the woman appeared to worry after flicking a glance over Dany.

Georgia's voice was petulant, though, as she said to Greg, "Don't tell me you're planning to work while you're here? Nobody will ever know if you take time to play instead. I'm sure Miss . . . er . . . your secretary"—she smiled brilliantly just for an instant in Dany's direction before turning back—"would like to have some time to herself."

Dany started to announce that she planned to have ten more days to herself and that she wasn't any happier about the situation than the brunette, but her lips had barely parted before Greg cut in.

"There's plenty of time for work and play," he told Georgia, letting his glance rest on Dany again as he said, "I would like to get together and discuss a few things with you. Maybe later on."

"Don't forget that you promised to have a drink with the Slaters before dinner," Georgia reminded him, reaching for her matching nylon cover-up at the foot of her lounge.

"I said I would if I could," Greg told her

pleasantly but firmly. Looking back to Dany, he said, "I've made dinner reservations for us here at seven. Is this place you're staying nearby?"

She should have told him that she was in a lodge ten miles down the road, except that she knew she wouldn't get away with it. The best thing was simply to be as noncommittal as possible. "Not far," she said tersely. "I can meet you in the lobby at seven if that's what you want. Now, if you'll excuse me . . ." She backtracked as gracefully as possible, saying, "It was nice meeting you, Mrs. Rowland."

The brunette looked up, as if surprised to find her still on the premises. "Yes, yes, of course." Her tone changed abruptly. "Greg—you're not leaving?"

"Just seeing Danielle on her way," he said.

Dany felt his hand come down with surprising firmness on her forearm as she started to protest, "It isn't necessary . . ."

"Nonsense. No trouble at all," he assured her, opening the glass door of the windbreak and shoving her ahead of him.

"I really don't need a guide," she said, finally managing to escape from his grasp when they reached the lodge door an instant later. "And you won't want to be away from your friend any longer than necessary."

He opened his mouth to object and then took a deep breath instead as he stared down at her, his eyes mere slits. "Your concern over my social life is touching. Are you always such a paragon?"

"Always," she said, trying to keep her tone as level as his. "But even paragons know when to tread lightly."

His brows drew together. "What is this—an early-warning system?"

"Of course not." She stared back at him reproachfully. "Mrs. Rowland is certainly gorgeous —I can see why any man would be attracted to her."

"Well, then, what's the problem?"

"I have the feeling she plays for keeps. And anybody who doesn't recognize the symptoms probably wears a coat with sleeves that buckle in the back." She watched color surge under his cheekbones with satisfaction and turned to go in the lodge. Before she could even take a step, she found herself dragged back to face him.

"If I want advice on my love life, I'll write to a lonely-hearts column," he gritted out. "And if you'd showed up on time today, I wouldn't have gotten trapped by that woman in the first place."

"I didn't even get your message until breakfast time, and it takes a while to get here from Yellowstone," she flared back, stung into defending herself. "Besides, I'm supposed to be on vacation." She clenched her hands at her sides, bracing to deliver her ultimatum. "This is as good a time as any to tell you that—"

Her employer cut in with devastating frankness before she could finish. "All I want to know now is exactly where you're staying. You just mentioned a phone number on your itinerary. Is it one of those condos overlooking the lake?"

A sneaked look at his determined features made Dany's rebellion fade. Especially when another brief glance showed that his brunette was standing up by the pool, obviously planning to come and protect her interests. "It's the condominium unit closest to the lake—third floor on the end," she muttered irritably. "The nameplate on the door says 'Abbott.'"

"That's all I wanted to know." Greg turned toward the pool again, saying casually over his shoulder, "I'll see you for dinner. You'd better get some rest before then."

Dany stared after him angrily before going back into the lodge and letting the door slam behind her. She caught a glimpse of her figure in the display glass of the lodge's gift shop and grimaced with annoyance. Her jeans were clean at least. So was her blouse—although it still had creases from being packed in the suitcase. But when it came to a contest with that brunette he'd dug up—she didn't have a prayer. Especially since Mrs. Rowland hadn't been wearing enough clothes for a wrinkle to have a chance!

"Did you find Mr. Fremont all right?" the girl behind the reception desk wanted to know as Dany stomped past.

"Oh, yes—I found him." She paused just long enough to ask, "What do people wear to dinner here?"

"Anything and everything," was the frank reply. The clerk smiled in friendly fashion as she added, "Actually, it's pretty informal except for some of the permanent residents of the resort who come in for dinner—then it's best bib and tucker."

"Thanks, I'll remember," Dany said, knowing very well that Greg's brunette would be one of the latter category.

She went over the contents of her suitcase mentally as she walked down to the resort shopping mall nearby. The best she could do was her pleated royal-blue faille, which fortunately came out of a bag looking the way it did when it went in. With a strand of baroque pearls at the high neckline and matching earrings, at least her appearance would be acceptable.

That thought reassured her and she went into the food store of the mall looking considerably more cheerful. She carefully chose some staples which would come in handy for the next guest at the condo as part of her hostess present. After going through the checkstand, she found the sack of groceries was heavier than she'd planned, and she clutched it in front of her with both arms as she went down the winding path toward the condominium units. A pretty creek ran alongside it, the shallow but rapid current finally emptying into the scenic artificial lake created by the resort's developers a mile away. Halfway down the path, Dany encountered a muddy patch brought about by recent rains and detoured around it with some concern, trying to keep her shoes dry. Unfortunately, the grass on the creek bank was long enough to hide a rough piece of ground and she stepped into a hole, losing her balance momentarily.

A round tin of Danish bacon jolted out of her grocery bag and rolled to the creek's edge in the process.

Dany mentioned a pithy phrase under her breath which told what she thought of that! She carefully put the rest of her groceries on a dry part of the path and edged her way down the steep grassy slope to retrieve the bacon. Everything went according to plan until she stooped to pick it up. Then the soggy rain-soaked bank crumbled under her weight and, an instant later, she found herself sitting in knee-deep water.

2

It had happened so fast and the dunking was so ridiculous that any other time she would have been convulsed with laughter. As it was, she could have wept in frustration. Jeans and walking shoes didn't dry overnight, and she was wearing the most vital parts of her vacation wardrobe. As she struggled to her feet and crawled inelegantly up the bank, she knew she'd either have to wear damp gear for the next day or so or deplete her vacation funds with unexpected shopping.

A quick glance around showed that at least no one had seen her stupid dunking, so she could be grateful for small mercies. She bent over to pick up the bag of groceries—trying to keep it away from her soggy shirt—and suddenly realized that she'd forgotten the can of bacon which had caused all the trouble. It took but a second to note that the bank was bare—apparently the can of bacon was now at the bottom of the creekbed, and it could damned well stay there!

31

She squelched her way to the condominium, trying to ignore the water trail she was leaving behind. It was harder to ignore the crisp wind which seemed to cut through her wet clothes like a lance. The icy gusts reminded her that she was at an elevation of 7,500 feet and the season was early fall. It was one thing to go swimming in the heated lodge pool surrounded by a glass windbreak; taking a plunge in the creek was a horse of another color.

And right then the horse's color was blue, Dany thought dismally as she finally reached the stairway which led up to her condominium. Once she reached the top and deposited her groceries against the door, she experienced a moment's panic before she discovered her nylon wallet and key case were still in her back pocket. The thought of her having to go back and search through the stream bed was not to be considered, and she sighed in relief as she unlocked the apartment door.

It was easiest to head straight for the kitchen linoleum, and once she'd shoved the groceries onto a counter, she decided to take off her clothes there as well. Her shivering didn't subside as she peeled down her nylon underthings, and she uttered a slight moan as she remembered that she hadn't turned on the electric heat before going over to the lodge.

An instant later, after a barefoot dash to the bathroom to find a towel and turn on the shower, another appalling fact came to mind; she'd also neglected to flip the switch for the water heater, so the cold water spurting from the shower was all she was apt to have for another twenty minutes.

By then she was so cold that her teeth were chattering, and she peeled off her wet underthings to scrub her body with the rough towel—hoping that increased circulation would help a little bit until she could at least heat a kettleful of water on the range.

She was so engrossed in her task that she barely heard the first ring of the doorbell. The second one was accompanied by the strong thumping of somebody's fist, so it was impossible to ignore. Probably it was the resident manager, who'd seen her car parked outside, she thought irritably as she wrapped the towel around her, sarong fashion and marched to the front door.

After putting on the chain guard, she opened it a bare inch and peered through the crack.

"Oh, no," she moaned as she saw Greg Fremont staring angrily back at her. "You can't come in," she said, and started to close the door.

He stopped that by the simple expedient of putting his shoulder against it. "Don't be ridiculous," he said. And then, after getting a better look at her shivering form, he added, "Open the door. Right now!"

The last two words were uttered with such force that Dany almost leapt to obey. It wasn't until after the chain came rattling free and he'd pushed the door wide that she wondered if she'd lost her mind.

She was determined to keep her dignity and found it almost impossible with the miserable towel coming adrift. "I'm trying to get dressed, so there's no point in your waiting—"

"What in the hell happened?" he interrupted after his glance had swept around the room.

Dany knew that he hadn't missed her jeans and blouse resting in a puddle on the kitchen linoleum along with her shoes. "I slipped," she said, hoping he'd let it go at that.

He didn't. "Into what?"

"The creek. C-r-e-e-k," she spelled it out for him, knowing she was being childish, but it was the way she felt just then. "And it was a damned cold creek, so I'm not in the mood to—"

"Did you take a hot shower?" he interrupted again.

"No."

"Why not?"

"Because there isn't any hot water and I didn't think a cold shower would help anything." She clutched the ends of the towel at her breast and started back toward the bathroom. "It's all right because— What are you doing?" The last came in a squeak as she felt his fingers hook into the back of her towel, almost dislodging it completely before she managed to drag it back into place.

"Don't walk away from me," he told her in a tone of voice that showed his glimpse of blue feminine flesh hadn't done a thing for his libido. If anything, his expression was more ominous than ever when she managed to turn and face him, still clutching the towel. "If there isn't any hot water here, put something on and we'll go where there is," he told her tersely. "This place feels like a barn—you'll never get warm."

"It'll be all right in a while. I've turned on the baseboard unit and found the switch panel for the water heater."

"Then it'll be ready for you later tonight," he said, going past her into the bedroom to find a short green velour robe atop her open suitcase. "Get into this while I find something for your feet." He continued his foraging into her suitcase. "These thongs should be okay." Turning with them in his hand, he scowled to find her still standing in the middle of the room clutching the velour robe. "What are you waiting for?" he wanted to know. "Can't you manage without help?"

As she saw him start purposefully toward her, she took an involuntary step back toward the bathroom. "Stay right there! I can't go anywhere wearing this, for heaven's sake."

"Why not? Georgia was wearing a lot less this afternoon."

"A bikini's different . . ."

"I *had* noticed," he said with irony. "It won't make a damn bit of difference what you've got on because there's a side door to the lodge right next to my room. I'll park by it and nobody will be any the wiser. While you're in a hot bath, I'll even come back here and bring you the missing parts of your wardrobe. But right now . . ."—he consulted the watch on his wrist—"I'm giving you thirty seconds to get into the robe, or I'll do it for you. Understand?"

"This is ridiculous . . ." She broke off when she saw his attention was still focused on the watch. She drew an exasperated breath and disappeared into the bathroom, slamming the door behind her.

It opened again, probably half a minute later, when she'd just finished buttoning the robe. Greg's glance went over her then, but he merely held out the thongs for her to slip on.

An instant later, she'd snatched a thin nylon raincoat from the closet and draped it around her shoulders en route to the front door. There wasn't any conversation while she trailed him down the steps to his car. The biting wind cut through her velour robe as if it were cheesecloth, and Dany wondered if she'd ever be warm again.

There was a brief respite once they got in the car, and Greg didn't waste any time accelerating back to the lodge, pulling up at a side door as he'd promised.

By then Dany wasn't concerned with what anyone thought about her strange attire and slipped out of the car quietly when he opened the door for her. An instant later, they were in a carpeted hall of the lodge, which was deserted except for a maid's cart at the other end.

Greg hurriedly unlocked his room and ushered

her ahead of him with a brusque gesture. As they went in, she saw him turn up the thermostat for the baseboard heat before heading straight for the bathroom to start running water in the tub. "Keep it as hot as you can stand it," he told her, coming out again. "I'll be out here for a little while if you need anything, and then you can tell me what you want me to bring you to wear for dinner."

"But you can't get back in the apartment . . ." She broke off as she saw him reach in his pocket and pull out her keys, which he'd apparently appropriated while she'd been in the bathroom at the condominium. "What do you do for an encore?"

If her sarcasm disconcerted him, he didn't let on. He merely jerked a thumb in the direction of the tub and left her to it.

The moment she stepped into the blissfully hot bath, she wondered why she'd put up such a fight. She let the water get as deep as possible and then sank down to her chin, making only a halfhearted attempt to keep her hair dry. The way she felt just then, she could spend the rest of the night in there.

It might have been ten minutes later or maybe even longer when there was a warning knock. Dany, who had been idly trying to turn the hot-water faucet with her toes, submerged abruptly as the bathroom door started to open.

Greg must have heard her agitated splashes because the door remained open only a crack as he said around it, "I'm going to get your things. Maybe it'll be easier if I just bring your suitcase. Is there anything hanging in the closet that you need for dinner?"

Dany steadied her voice with an effort. "There's a royal-blue dress—if it's not too much trouble."

"I think I can manage," came his dry reply. There was a pause; then he asked, "Are you finally getting warm?"

"Yes, thanks." Dany's sense of humor came to the fore as she added, "It's too bad that room service doesn't come tubside—"

"You might have a problem with the lodge waiters, but I'd be glad to oblige. . . ."

Dany thought she saw the door open wider and sank to chin level again, saying breathlessly, "Never mind, thanks. I'll be out by the time you get back."

"I thought you might be." There was no attempt to hide the amusement in his voice before he closed the door again. An instant later Dany heard him go out into the hallway.

She waited a moment longer to make sure the coast was clear and then reluctantly got out of the tub, reaching for one of the big bath towels to dry herself. After using it vigorously, she lingered in front of the mirror to smooth her hair and then blotted the damp ends with a dry towel from the rack.

When the phone rang, her first impulse was to

ignore the interruption. Then, as it continued, she reached for her velour robe; she wasn't taking any chances on Greg finding her swathed in another damp towel!

An instant later she picked up the phone and uttered a cautious hello. There was a pause and then a feminine voice at the other end of the wire said, just as cautiously, "I was calling Mr. Fremont's room."

"This *is* Mr. Fremont's room," Dany said, frowning again as she saw that she'd left a trail of damp footprints on the rug.

"Well, may I speak to him, please." The voice sounded much crisper.

"I'm sorry—he isn't here." Dany's businesslike self took over then. "Could I take a message for him? He shouldn't be long."

"Oh, wouldn't you know!" There was exasperation in the clear, brisk tones. "I'm just between planes, so he can't phone me. Tell him Sylvia called, please. And be sure to let him know that I was able to get a seat on his flight from Bozeman later this week, as we planned, so I'll see him then. Do you have all that?"

"You'll be on the flight that he's taking from Bozeman later this week." Dany wanted very much to ask where that flight was going, but the unknown Sylvia probably would be reluctant to volunteer the information and she really couldn't blame her. Probably *she* was wondering who in the dickens Dany was and didn't dare ask.

"Yes—well, you won't forget to tell him," Sylvia asked, clearly uneasy about getting the word through.

"I expect Mr. Fremont shortly," Dany said, taking pity on her because the woman sounded very nice. It wasn't her fault that she didn't know Greg Fremont counted his female acquaintances in bunches like carrots. "Don't worry," she went on, "I'll make sure he gets the message."

She hung up with the other still uttering effusive thanks, because there was suddenly a light knocking from the hallway. Probably Greg was so busy remembering to take her keys that he forgot his own, she thought as she made sure her velour robe was fastened properly and opened the door.

Encountering Georgia Rowland's surprised glance an instant later, she knew that she'd been judged guilty without even a trial.

The brunette was dressed to the nines in a clinging violet chiffon that was more suited to Manhattan than Montana but probably the entire male population of Big Sky would have debated that. "I thought this was Greg's room," she said, sounding annoyed as she tried to see into the bedroom beyond Dany's figure.

"It is," Dany said, "but he isn't here right now."

The other's glance went swiftly over Dany's robe, which clung damply, evidence that there wasn't anything under it other than skin. Georgia's frown deepened and she said, "He's joining us for cocktails. It seemed sensible to go down to the bar together."

"Of course, perhaps you'd like to come in and wait," Dany said, keeping a straight face. "He shouldn't be long—he just went over to bring me some clothes."

If looks could have killed, Dany would have collapsed on the spot. Color surged under Georgia's cheekbones at that remark and she drew herself up to full height. "No, thanks," she said stiffly. "When Greg can tear himself away, I'll see him in the bar."

One up to the home team, Dany thought with wry satisfaction as she closed the door after Georgia had disappeared down the hall. A month ago she wouldn't have engaged in that verbal sparring match. She acknowledged the sobering truth to her reflection in the bathroom mirror and decided that was what working for a man like Greg did to a woman. If she didn't put a healthy distance between them soon she'd make a habit of clawing and scratching.

A brisk knock and then the sound of a key in the hall door announced the object of her trouble, and she marched out to meet him, her chin at a determined angle.

He was depositing her suitcase on a luggage rack near the door and turned to face her, her blue dress still on its hanger over his arm. "I think I remembered everything," he began, and then hesitated as he noted her stormy expression. "Anything wrong?"

"Not at all." Dany found it was difficult to maintain her dignity in bare feet and wearing only a velour housecoat. "Everything is just fine."

"You finally got warm?"

She could have told him she was seething—after serving as a message center for the past five minutes. "Yes, thanks." She brushed past him to snatch up a handful of underthings and some stockings under his masculine gaze. "You missed a phone call from Sylvia," she said, wishing to heaven she could locate her cosmetic bag without going through her entire suitcase. "She didn't give her last name."

"I don't know that many Sylvias," he said levelly. "Did she leave a number?"

"No. She was between flights." Dany kept her glance on the jumbled suitcase so she wouldn't have to dwell on the contrast between his immaculate blue blazer and charcoal slacks and her own disheveled state. "She said to tell you that she'd gotten space on your flight from Bozeman—as you planned."

"Good." Greg consulted his watch and turned toward the door. "Anything else?" he wanted to know.

"You had a caller." Dany knew that she was sounding prim and unpleasant but she couldn't help herself. "Your brunette—from the pool. To guide you to the bar. In case you missed your way."

"Kind of her." From his tone, Greg could have

been discussing the possibility of rain before morning. "I must remember to thank her."

"She seemed a little upset at finding me here. . . ."

He paused with the hall door halfway open to glance over his shoulder. "I don't suppose you explained," he said softly.

Her gaze faltered before his. "I . . . I . . . No, I didn't," she said finally on a defiant breath.

"Then I'll have to salvage your reputation. I'll meet you in the dining room in an hour. Don't be late. And don't waste any time going back to that apartment of yours. You might as well stay here."

"I don't see why . . ." she began, and found she was addressing the wooden door which he'd closed firmly behind him.

It was just as well she hadn't argued any longer, Dany thought. If Greg went on safari with that look on his face, even lions would lock their doors.

She caught sight of her reflection in the mirror above a long bureau and grimaced. It was a good thing she'd combed her hair, because the rest of the scenery wasn't anything to write home about. At least she could improve the terrain, she thought as she slowly undid her robe. She couldn't compete with Georgia's violet-chiffon creation, but she wouldn't look like a poor relation.

If the masculine reaction when she walked past the bar exactly an hour later was any indication, apparently she'd succeeded. There was a low whistle from the man sitting on a stool nearby and a satisfactory break in the conversation among a group just beyond. A small smile played around Dany's lips, but she kept her gaze fixed on the maitre d' standing at the door of the dining room just beyond.

"I'm joining Mr. Fremont," she began, and then broke off as Greg approached from a side room to take her arm.

"If you'll follow me," the maitre d' murmured, and led them across the high-ceilinged room to a table next to the floor-to-ceiling windows which covered one entire wall.

"I hope I didn't make you cut your party short," Dany said politely to Greg once the man had left them with menus and a promise to send their waiter right over.

"I was glad to leave," Greg said. "Making conversation with a bunch of strangers isn't my idea of fun. No matter how pleasant they are." The last comment was a drawled afterthought as he opened his menu.

Dany tried to think of something nice to say on the subject of his poolside acquaintances and failed, so she kept quiet, trying to look as if the dinner entrees were the only things that interested her just then.

Apparently Greg's attention wasn't limited to the printed page because he said, "You've achieved quite a transformation in an hour. That dress didn't look half as good on the hanger.

Maybe you should take an ice-water plunge every afternoon." He paused before going on. "All the same, you'd better have an early night. And you won't have to worry about being warm—I turned the thermostat all the way up when I was over at the condo."

"In that case, I'd better send an extra-nice hostess present with my thank-you letter. Or maybe just a check for her electric bill."

Obviously that problem hadn't occurred to him, because he frowned at her over the top of the menu. "Are you serious?"

"Not really. I'm only here overnight, so it won't be a problem."

"That's what I want to talk to you about . . ." His expression lightened momentarily. "Not bankruptcy—but about the length of your stay. Never mind—let's order first." The last came as a waiter approached. "What sounds good to you? I understand the trout is a specialty here, but frankly I'd rather have roast beef."

They settled the important question of food and were served with a generous portion of green salad and piping-hot-from-the-oven French bread before he went back to his original topic. "It would be more convenient for me if you stayed over a day or so—"

"But I'm on my way home." Her eyebrows drew together as she surveyed him across the beige linen tablecloth. "Miss Snyder should have told you."

"I knew you were going to the Hells Canyon

area—that's why I arranged to meet you here."
He frowned at her uncomprehending face.
"Didn't she mention that I'm going there too?
Later this week."

"The only person who told me anything was
your friend Sylvia—on the phone. And the sum
total of her news was that you're sharing an airplane," Dany said curtly. "It wasn't a very long
conversation."

"You should have made it last a little longer—
it might have paid off." He surveyed her carefully. "No questions?"

Dany could have furnished a whole page of
them at that point, but she only shook her head.

"You're too good to be true. If I didn't know
better after seeing you dunked and dripping this
afternoon, I'd think you were missing some vital
parts."

Dany bunched her napkin and put it beside her
plate. "Even roast beef isn't worth this. If you'll
excuse me—"

"Sit down." Greg didn't raise his voice, but
there was something in his tone that made her
flop back into her chair. "Don't be a damned
fool," he went on. "I don't pay you to be a hyster-
ical female with a temper tantrum every five
minutes."

"Make up your mind." She matched his
irritable tone. "One minute I'm a natural wonder
and the next I'm a total loss." Her hands went
out in a helpless gesture. "I don't even know why
I'm here—unless you want some local color on the

Hells Canyon area. And you should have asked me about it before you made your reservations, because I don't think it's your kind of place at all."

"At least we agree about that. So far as I'm concerned, the trip is strictly business," Greg said, taking a sip of water.

"But what about Sylvia—I mean, the woman who phoned?" Dany asked impulsively before she realized that it wasn't really any of her affair.

Fortunately, Greg chose to overlook that fact. "What about her?"

"Well, I just meant that some women wouldn't be happy to be fitted in—as sort of an afterthought. Oh, you know what I'm trying to say," she finished in a rush.

"You have a decided talent for getting the wrong end of the stick," he said as he buttered some bread and took a bite. "Sylvia," he went on before she could interrupt, "is a good friend of mine, but she's also a top-flight accountant. That's why she's joining the trip."

"I see." Dany narrowed her eyes thoughtfully as she stared down at the tablecloth.

"Now what?" Greg asked, sounding resigned.

"I just wondered who had retained you. There aren't too many big outfits left in the area. Three or four ranches and only two resort spreads."

He placed his knife alongside his fork on the plate with more force than necessary. "I'm going to a place called White Water Lodge, and since it's your home ground, I thought you could give me a helping hand in the general operations . . . What's the matter?" He broke off as he noticed that she'd remained motionless, her fork halfway to her lips.

"You mean you've been retained by someone at White Water?"

He nodded, still puzzled. Then he reached inside his jacket to pull out a paper from an inside pocket. "Evan Monroe, to be explicit. I understand he's the general manager of the operation and plans to sell out. He wants advice on how to handle the tax ramifications on the transaction."

Dany concentrated on putting her fork down carefully on the edge of the plate, trying to hide her trembling fingers.

Greg half-rose to his feet, leaning concernedly over the table. "You're not going to pass out, are you? What the hell's happening?"

"You're stealing my line." Dany managed a quirky smile as she leaned back in her chair. "Evan Monroe is my stepfather. The lodge belonged to my mother's family and he swore on a stack of Bibles that he had no plans to sell it."

"I didn't know or I'd certainly never have sprung the news to you like this," Greg said, his eyebrows an ominous line across his forehead. "It's always a wrench when there's a decision to sell family property—but your stepfather must think that he's doing the right thing."

"I hope so."

Her words were so terse that his frown grew even more pronounced as he stared at her troubled face. "What's that supposed to mean?"

"Because my mother died before she could change her will and cut him out of the property. They'd only been married six months. At least I know now why Evan sounded so stricken after I phoned and said that I was arriving this week. He probably thought I'd gotten wind of his maneuvering and . . ."

"   . . . that you'd put the cat among the pigeons?"

Her smile didn't hold the slightest vestige of humor. "Something like that. It's a temptation."

His expression didn't give anything away as he stared at her. "Are you going to?"

Dany's quizzical smile didn't reach her eyes as her gaze held his across the table. Then she only said one word, drawling it out in tomcat style. "Meow."

3

There was a pattern to the goings-on and it wasn't any use trying to deny it.

Three days after her early-morning departure from Big Sky, Dany found herself once again hurrying to keep an appointment with Greg. At least this time it was on her home ground, she told herself as she drove carefully through the lingering early-morning darkness toward the big Hellsgate Marina on the Snake River. Behind her the lights in Lewiston were just starting to come on as the residents of the Idaho town girded themselves for another day.

Since Dany had just arrived late the evening before, she hadn't done much except find a motel and fall into bed. Fortunately, the place boasted a twenty-four-hour coffee shop, so after responding to her early wake-up call, she was able to have toast and coffee before starting on her drive to the marina.

Even though the scenic road was narrow and winding, following the contours of the big river, the territory was so familiar that Dany made her way instinctively, her mind mainly occupied with the events which had brought her there.

They hadn't lingered over dinner at Big Sky after Greg had made his announcement. He seemed to sense that Dany's shock at his news went deep, and he had pointedly avoided the subject of Hells Canyon during the rest of the meal. When they'd finished their coffee he announced that she probably wanted an early night after all that had happened, and marched her back to his room. They'd collected her belongings without wasting a minute and then he'd driven her back to her borrowed condominium. He stood inside the door there long enough to make sure that the interior was warm before setting a date to meet her at the Hellsgate Marina in Idaho later on.

"That way your stepfather won't have to make more than one pickup," he'd said, keeping his hand on the doorknob so she wouldn't get any wrong ideas. "I understand there's quite a distance involved between the marina and the lodge."

Dany kept her voice carefully level. "About fifty miles."

Greg had looked startled at that and then nodded again. "Then there's certainly no need for him to make two trips. Unless it conflicts with any of your plans."

It was a temptation to tell him what he and Sylvia and her stepfather could do with their plans. Then she recalled her anemic bank balance. She also knew that she'd gotten in the habit of eating three meals a day, so it wasn't the time to make precipitate gestures.

"You needn't answer that."

Greg's words came dimly to her ears, and she frowned, trying to remember what he'd said. "I beg your pardon?"

"You couldn't make it much plainer that your vacation has turned out to be a total frost," he said, looking grim again. "Believe me, I didn't know that this White Water Lodge project had anything to do with you. Maybe it would be better if you joined forces with me and we flew to Hells Canyon together. It would save you a long drive by yourself."

A long drive was far preferable to playing an unwanted third with him and his Sylvia, Dany thought. To say nothing of another day of staying at Big Sky with the strikingly beautiful Georgia for competition. It was easier to bow out while she had an excuse. "I'm used to driving—it doesn't bother me. Besides, I may need a car later."

"What are you dreaming up now?" Greg didn't bother to hide the impatience in his tone.

"Well, I certainly won't want to hang around the lodge. Once I collect some of my belongings that I left stored there, I'll be on my way. Evan and I don't really get along."

"I'd prefer to have you stay," Greg said, sounding like an impatient employer again. "Your step-father's still an unknown quantity to me."

"And I'm not?" The dispassionate way Greg was looking at her made Dany's response flat.

"Let's just say that I'm beginning to catch on to what makes you tick. As much as you'll let me." He leaned against the door frame to study her with his usual insouciance. "Now I'm wondering if it's a case of still water running deep or—"

"Just stagnant," she cut in before he could finish. "No hidden currents or white-water drama. All you had to do was ask."

"There you go again." He shot a glance at his watch. "Hell! This isn't the time for philosophic dissertations. Not if you insist on making that long drive."

"How nice to find that we *do* agree on something," she said sweetly.

"We'll consider the topic postponed—not abandoned." There was an undercurrent of steel in his voice as he stepped out onto the porch. "Will I see you for breakfast?"

"I doubt it. There's a good place to eat at Three Rivers and it's just sixty miles down the road." She walked over to the door and started to ease it shut.

"Not so fast." His sturdy black loafer kept the door open. "Where *will* I see you, then?"

"Well, if you're serious about combining forces —Lewiston's Hellsgate Marina is the starting point on the river. Since we're arriving on a

Wednesday, we'll have to catch the mail-boat run."

"Your stepfather mentioned an early-morning departure in his letter."

"That's right." Dany's lips curved suddenly in a wicked smile. "On mail-boat days that means seven o'clock from the dock."

Greg winced; obviously he hadn't planned on having to get up at dawn. She knew he'd be even less enthusiastic after changing planes to get to Lewiston in the first place.

"I have the feeling," he said slowly, "that there are quite a few aspects of this project that your stepfather forgot to mention. Are you sure that you wouldn't rather fly west with me? We could have someone take care of your car. That way, we could get a few things settled before we arrived." His glance flicked to the empty apartment behind her and then came back. "For one thing, you wouldn't have to go to bed quite so early—unless you wanted to."

"As part of getting a few things settled?" She kept her voice bland.

"I thought you'd understand." He didn't try to hide his amusement then.

"Oh, I do. Unfortunately"—she crossed her fingers behind her skirt—"it doesn't appeal to me."

He straightened slowly in the doorway. "You can't tell until you try. Why don't you crawl down off that pillar of outraged femininity and act like a human being for a change?"

"Because I'd find myself standing in line behind Georgia tonight and Sylvia the day your plane comes in," she snapped, her eyes sparkling with annoyance. "At least on a pillar I won't get mowed down by your admiring entourage. I'm sorry not to cooperate, but the evening hasn't been a total loss—you can put my dinner check down as a sales expense."

He withdrew his foot from the edge of the door. "Only one thing wrong with that—I won't list it as a sales expense. Strictly a frozen asset." Then he was gone before she could think of a suitable reply.

His comment still rankled in Dany's thoughts three days later and she pushed it to the back of her mind with an effort as she turned onto the side road marked "Hellsgate Marina."

There were pink streaks crisscrossing the sky when she drove into the big deserted parking lot close to the pier where the familiar jet boat fleet was anchored.

She turned off the engine and opened the door, standing beside the car to sniff eagerly at the fresh breeze from the wide gray waters of the Snake. Ten miles up, the canyon would narrow and the currents would turn turbulent, but at Hellsgate there was a serenity broken only by a flock of water birds as they swooped over the grassy slopes of the recreation area and then swept on. They seemed to investigate the rows of pleasure boats moored at the farthest pier and then disappeared against the still-hazy morning sky.

An approaching car brought Dany's attention to the roadway leading down to the marina and, as she identified the outlines of a van, she smiled and closed her car door.

The van's driver let out two staccato blasts of the horn as he pulled up beside her, leaning out the window to say, "I should have known you'd beat me here. Stay where you are, girl." The last came as he shut off the ignition and jumped down to the pavement. He hurried around the front of the van without even bothering to close his door and swept Dany into a strong, bearlike embrace. His first kiss was brief and enthusiastic; the second one lasted so long that she had to push away to finally get her breath. "Jeff, for heaven's sake!" she gasped. Then a glance up at his satisfied features made her laugh and shake her head. "You've been practicing since I've been away."

"I thought you might notice the difference," Jeff Coates said complacently.

Dany let her gaze wander over him, admiring his tall spare form, which was only a few pounds heavier than when she'd first met him years before. He was a senior in college then and working as a freight roustabout on the river. His fair hair was worn a little longer these days and his features had fined down in the ensuing four years, but otherwise he looked about the same. There was the same reckless twinkle in his pale blue eyes and a deceptive strength to his wiry frame. Two years before, he'd signed on as an assistant at the lodge, helping out with maintenance mainly but serving as an official meeter and greeter when the summer tours were the heaviest. Jeff merely had to flash his grin to make the women under twenty-five blink and cluster round. Later on, her stepfather used the same tactic with the older women.

"Satisfied?" There was an assurance in Jeff's voice, as if he'd been waiting for her approval.

"I'm impressed," Dany told him, her smile matching his. "Even at this hour of the morning."

"You're not the only one." He dragged his glance away to check his watch. "Damn! We should be leaving now, and we're still missing some passengers. That is, if your Greg Fremont is coming. He hasn't changed his mind, has he?"

"When I saw him a couple of days ago in Montana, he hadn't." She frowned then as she saw him reach back into the van and drag out two mail sacks and an assortment of parcels. "Are you doing the mail route today?"

Jeff nodded. "Chuck's down with flu. He's on the mend but still wasn't up to the trip. Can you give me a hand with some of this?"

"I'll be glad to. Shall I put my bags aboard first?" She nodded toward her neatly stacked belongings near the path.

"Don't bother. I'll pick those up when we get this stuff." He was piling parcels in her arms as he spoke.

"Which boat are we taking?"

"The small one." He jerked his chin toward the

long pier in front of them, where two aluminum jet boats were tied up. "We don't need any extra space, since there'll just be five of us."

"Five?" It was hard for Dany to turn her head to question him, since the last big parcel reached her chin. "I thought there'd be four."

"Well, there's your Mr. Fremont and his particular baggage. A woman called Logan—according to your stepdad. And you, of course."

"Together with you—that still makes four."

"Actually, it'll be four and a half. Chuck and his wife sent their baby girl down to Grandma's while he's been sick. He's a freight handler at the bar this season when he's not doing the mail run. Now that he's almost well, it's safe for her at home and Grandma's sending her back. I didn't think you'd mind baby-sitting for an hour."

"Of course not." Dany fell into step beside him as he lugged two mail bags down to the boat. "When's Grandma coming?"

"Any minute, I hope. On a mail run, I don't drag my feet, or the taxpayers upriver complain."

"I can't blame them," Dany said, pulling up at the edge of the pier alongside a serviceable work boat of some thirty feet with the unoriginal name of *River Belle*. There was a metal canopy over the wheelhousing, but the stern part of the little craft was uncovered, allowing passengers who sat on two rows of metal seats an unobstructed view of the mighty river and, later on, the spine-tingling stretches of white water.

Dany watched Jeff shove his mail bags under

the wheel and then handed over her load of packages, which he put carefully in a storage area at the bow. She noticed several cartons of groceries already stowed away and said, "This looks like a grocery run, too."

"Evan and I knew we'd have to restock the larder, since we'll have company. We've let the stores get a little thin the last week or so."

Dany looked over his well-muscled form with amusement. "You don't look as if you've missed many calories lately."

"Well, to be honest, I haven't. Both of us took a break from the lodge last week and decided to try our luck in Reno." As he swung over the railing and came back up beside her on the pier, his glance was rueful. "I would have done better to have stayed home."

"That's what happens to me, too. I'm just surprised that you were able to get away at this time of year. The reservations must be way off."

He shrugged and started back up to collect her luggage, saying over his shoulder, "You know how it is near the end of the season. Besides, Evan is trying mainly for convention groups and seminars these days rather than bothering with individual reservations."

So not only had her stepfather decided to sell the lodge, Dany gathered, he wasn't even trying to dazzle potential buyers with an imposing financial statement. Such goings-on wouldn't impress Greg, with his expertise in handling commercial property transactions.

Jeff interrupted her thoughts when he came back with her bags and went aboard the *Belle* to store them forward alongside the groceries. "You can't be planning to stay long," he commented, straightening again after he'd finished. "I thought women carried everything like hermit crabs when they traveled."

She didn't rise to the bait, saying idly, "We're all different. I hate to drag suitcases around. Besides, unless things have changed upriver, a clean shirt and jeans should cover the social schedule." She cocked her head to give him a considering glance. "Don't tell me I'm going to need an apron too? Is Evan between cooks at the lodge?"

Jeff hurriedly reassured her. "Of course not. Evan found Hazel through some friends of his— she came highly recommended."

"I see." Dany decided that his answer was too glib. "How long have you had her?"

"Well . . ." He drew the word out. "Actually just a short time, but she must be okay. Hey, there's Chuck's mother-in-law and the baby," he said with what sounded like relief. "I'll go up and get her. When did you say that boss of yours was coming?"

"I didn't," Dany called after him, and then shrugged as she saw that his attention was on the pleasant middle-aged woman who was getting out of the car at the edge of the parking lot. She waved cheerily at Dany before she stooped back in the vehicle and extracted a baby from the car seat. The infant was deposited in Jeff's waiting arms and she searched on the rear seat to pull out a bulging diaper bag with a shoulder strap. She hung that over Jeff's free hand. Evidently she knew that Jeff was anxious to start up-river, because she didn't waste any time dropping a kiss on the baby's cheek before getting back in the car and driving off.

Jeff handled his new cargo with the same aplomb as he'd managed the other. "Dany—meet Liza," he said as he came down the pier again. "If you get aboard, you can hold her."

"In other words, sit down and get to work," Dany commented wryly, and then spoiled it by adding, "Isn't she a sweetie? How old is she?" as the fair-haired little girl showed an enchanting smile which revealed three tiny teeth.

"Almost a year." Manlike, Jeff was above such discussions. "You'd better sit under the canopy with her. It's warmer out of the wind and that snowsuit of hers, or whatever it is, isn't very thick." He waited until Dany had steadied herself aboard the craft and then handed the baby over the rail. The diaper bag was dropped carelessly at the other end of the seat.

Jeff glanced at his watch again and said, "Boss or no boss, I'm not going to wait more than five minutes longer. He can charter another boat if he's going to drag his feet like this." Then, as Dany sat down quickly on a metal seat so that she could try to disengage little Liza's grip from her ear, Jeff said, "I forgot to warn you—she likes noses, too . . . and watches." The last was added when ten baby fingers moved like lightning up to Dany's watchband.

Dany grinned back at the baby even though her ear still throbbed. "Listen, you little menace—it's too early in the morning for such maneuvers. Are you sure you don't want to have your Uncle Jeff hang on to you?"

Jeff shook his head and stayed safely out of reach on the pier. "As captain of this vessel, I'm giving the orders. . . ."

"Coward!"

"Just old enough to know better. That kid is busier than a beehive. Better watch that pendant of yours."

"Oh, help! Jeff—get her to let go so I can take it off."

"Okay, hang on." He vaulted over the rail and patiently pried the baby's fingers loose, while Liza let out a little crow of laughter. "She thinks this is some kind of game," he commented. "Lean closer so I can unhook the clasp of this chain, Dany—they make these fastenings damned small."

They were both so engrossed in trying to salvage her gold chain that the slamming of a car door nearby made them start with surprise.

Jeff looked over his shoulder to see the newest arrival. "Can't be for us," he said, turning back to Dany. "We're expecting a twosome."

She shifted the baby in her arms and peered past her head. One look at Greg's scowling features made her heart sink to her shoetops. "Don't you believe it—that's my boss." Her arms tightened nervously around the little girl as Greg came down the concrete pier. Liza, deprived of the gold chain, let out an outraged howl which gained in volume as she worked at it.

"Oh, hell!" Jeff said, caught halfway over the rail on his way to greet his newest passenger. He glanced down at Dany and flapped his hands. "Can't you keep her quiet?"

"What did you say?" Dany called back, trying to transfer the baby to her shoulder so that she could pat her back and soothe her.

"He asked if you couldn't keep her quiet," Greg said, biting his words off. He stopped alongside the boat and dropped his bag on the pier with a thud. "What the devil's going on here? Who does that baby belong to?"

"Her name's Liza—" Dany began, when Jeff cut in.

"My name's Coates. Jeff Coates. I'll be taking you upriver."

Greg frowned at Jeff's outstretched hand before finally putting out his own to shake it. "Monroe mentioned you in his letter. I'm Greg Fremont." And then, as if getting back to more important things, his glance settled on Dany again. "You didn't answer me. Who does that baby belong to?"

Liza stopped howling for an instant, as if surprised by this new creature, and Dany said quickly, "I'm not sure. Some people who live halfway upriver. Liza's been with her grandmother."

"Her dad's a freight handler who lives at our first stop," Jeff put in, clearly puzzled as to why Greg was harping on the child. "She won't be in the way for long—if that's what's bothering you."

Greg's obvious annoyance was as chilly as the wind whipping down the pier. "It's not bothering me. I was"—his attention flickered over Dany, who was cuddling the little girl in her arms again —"I was surprised, that's all."

"Well, you're not the only one," Jeff said, only partially mollified. "I thought you were bringing a lady with you. We can't wait any longer. On mail days—"

"She isn't coming until later this afternoon," Greg cut in calmly.

"—we have to keep to a schedule," Jeff kept going on until the other words sank in.

He paused for an instant then, and Dany asked what they both wanted to know. "You mean Jeff will have to make another trip?" She sounded doubtful. "There's a lot of distance involved, and it's difficult to make a pickup on time. I should have warned you. . . ."

"There's no problem. I've already made other arrangements for Sylvia."

Greg was back to his imperturbable manner, Dany thought, giving him a sidelong look as she sank down on one of the metal benches at the stern. Under the guise of settling the baby in her lap, she was able to watch him oversee the stowing of his gear in the forward area. He had a knack for wearing the right things at the right time, she decided. His clean but worn beige corduroy trousers fitted with scarcely a wrinkle, and there was a blue oxford-cloth sport shirt just visible beneath his padded zipper jacket. Even his shoes were sturdy leather boat shoes with a thick sole. Without even trying, he was fitting into the rugged surroundings as effortlessly as Jeff. And better than she was just then, she decided, when a sudden gust of wind rippled the water and cut through her suede jacket. At least her slacks were wool and she had a thick sweater in her case if Jeff gave her time to unearth it.

From the businesslike way he was starting the engine at that moment, she thought it would be better to shiver a little longer. He didn't look any happier than Greg did. As a matter of fact, little Liza, who'd reached over and found a cord on the seat and was joyously batting it against the railing, was the only person aboard who seemed content with her lot.

Dany managed to absorb the warmth of the infant's snowsuit as she shifted on the seat, finding a place that had a partial sheltering from the wind as Jeff kept the engine at idling speed when he went forward to release the bowline. Without asking, Greg positioned himself by the stern and handled the stern line as Jeff nodded. An instant later, Jeff was revving the jet engine and the *Belle* was on her way out of the marina.

In no time at all, Jeff had maneuvered the small

craft around the breakwater and then Dany felt the thrust as he used full jet power going up the center of the wide Snake River.

The whining noise made little Liza blink, and Dany quickly diverted her with the drawstring on a canvas bag Jeff had left on the edge of the seat. Greg made his way up to the wheel, giving her another of his raking glances when he passed her seat. Evidently he wasn't going to bother with sharing the baby-sitting chores, Dany deduced, and her lips twitched unwillingly.

Over the roar of the engines and Liza's babyish chirpings, she was only able to hear odds and ends of Jeff and Greg's conversation. It sounded as if Jeff was giving the usual answers about the small boat's capabilities. "Only draws eight inches," he was saying, and then, "aluminum is better than fiberglass for river work—this stuff will bend if you hit a submerged rock." Greg must have asked about the dangers of the river because Jeff went on at some length about high water being the most treacherous. "You can't see the rocks," he said. "The turbulence stirs up mud and debris. What you really have to watch out for in white water is getting a branch in the intake—cuts your power by ninety percent. In some places upriver, that's not good."

At that point, little Liza tired of the drawstring and tried to get to her feet in Dany's lap. When Dany held her tight, she squirmed even more vigorously and started to cry.

Her protests rose even over the noise of the jet engine, and Greg turned to see what the trouble was. Jeff took his glance from the river long enough to scowl over his shoulder and shout, "We've got another twenty minutes, Dany. Can't you keep her quiet? Maybe there's something in that bag of hers that I stowed away."

"I'll get it," Greg said, interpreting Jeff's gesture toward the storage area.

"It's that blue one on top of the pile," Jeff said, settling down on his seat behind the wheel again.

Greg braced himself against the metal wheel-housing, reaching for the diaper bag as Jeff kept his full speed up the powerful river. If Liza hadn't been squirming so energetically in her arms, Dany would have been admiring the tinge of green on the rugged grayish-brown hills on either side. At that part, the canyon was still broad and gave little evidence of the deep forbidding landscape it was to become farther up the river.

Liza wasn't in the least interested in the scenery and the volume of her sobs almost drowned out the jet engines in Dany's ears. "It's all right, sweetie," Dany tried to soothe her, and then shot a desperate look at Greg, who'd rested the diaper bag on the end of the seat to paw through it. "For heaven's sake! There must be something in there to help."

His glance was assessing. "It depends on which end you want to treat first."

"Which end? What on earth are you talking

about? . . . No, love—let go." Dany's last instruction was to Liza, who'd found a stray lock of hair and managed to get both her tiny fists on it.

"Here—let me." Greg's tone showed that he didn't think much of the status quo. He reached over to loosen the baby's clasp and then swung her up into his arms.

"She might be wet," Dany said, with a worried appraisal of Liza's derriere.

"Then you'd better go for that end. There are some diapers in the side of the bag. Was that what you wanted to hear, honey?" He addressed the small bundle in his arms, who had miraculously stopped her howling at his last words. "Poor kid," he added virtuously to Dany, "all you have to do is use a little common sense."

"In that case, you'd better handle the changing routine," she began after pulling out a disposable diaper. "I'd hate to interfere with an expert."

"Nonsense. This is a good time for you to pick up a few tips." Greg put Liza down on the narrow metal bench as he spoke, holding her safely with a strong arm. "Besides, using this thing as a changing table, it'll probably take both of us."

Dany didn't argue. From the way Liza was looking up at them with a quivering lower lip, the blessed silence wasn't going to last long. She peeled off the baby's outer garment, knowing she was all thumbs and aware that her lack of talent wasn't going unnoticed. At last she managed to remove a soggy diaper, dropping it onto the floor before unfolding the new one.

"You should have had that one ready," Greg commented critically. "Get on with it—this air's cold!"

"If you think you can do better . . ." Dany flared back, and then broke off as she saw Greg half-turn and start rooting in the diaper bag with his free hand. "What are you doing now?" she asked irritably when she discovered she had the bottom side of the diaper at Liza's waist and had to change things around. "Damn!"

"It's okay, honey," Greg was soothing little Liza, and waved a small bottle in front of her intent gaze. "There are better times ahead."

Dany finally managed to fasten the diaper properly, hoping to heaven that it wouldn't fall off before she could snap the tot's creeper. She achieved that before Greg could comment on her efforts, and finally got Liza bundled up again.

Greg didn't waste any time plunking the infant back in Dany's lap. "You *can* manage this, I presume?" he asked calmly, handing over the bottle of apple juice, which was providentially equipped with a nipple.

"I've already had breakfast. But don't let me stop you."

"Very funny." He shoved the bottle into her hands. "You'd better hurry up—Liza's losing patience."

Dany heard the warning whimper from the little girl in her arms and knew that Greg was right again. "It's all right, Liza," she said hastily, and managed to fit the nipple into the proper place without any more catastrophes.

With Liza cooperating fully, Dany watched half the juice diappear. She yanked the bottle out when Liza coughed once, and patted her instinctively.

"It's all right," Greg said, watching her.

"But she's starting to cry again . . ."

"Because she wants the rest of the juice," he said with terrible patience. "Look, do you want me to take over?"

Dany hesitated, knowing it was a no-win situation—no matter what she answered. The baby's protests, increasing in volume, decided the issue. "Maybe you'd better."

Greg sat down beside her and took Liza in his arms without a waste motion. The bottle was plugged in again and the baby relaxed, managing to look up at him adoringly—a maneuver she hadn't used earlier, Dany thought with some amusement.

"If you don't have anything else to do, you might get some of those crackers out for a second course," Greg said in a businesslike tone.

"Crackers?"

"Obviously you were an only child." He jerked his chin toward the end of the bench. "The ones in that bag of hers. You can't miss them."

Jeff took his eyes from his piloting long enough to watch her make her way toward the bag, and said, "You really take all that liberation stuff seriously, don't you?" He rubbed the side of his nose with a callused finger. "S'funny. I didn't think you were the type."

Dany stopped pawing through the bag long enough to give him a puzzled look. "What in the dickens are you talking about?"

He jerked his head toward Greg, who was competently disposing of the empty juice bottle while keeping Liza snug in the crook of his arm. "What have you got against taking care of a baby?"

"Oh, for heaven's sake! You just have to have two to keep her quiet. And there aren't any crackers in here . . ." She broke off as she encountered a plastic bag. "Yes, there are—graham crackers. Why didn't somebody tell me?"

"Were you expecting hardtack?"

She sent him a withering look and then had to clutch the back of a seat as the boat skittered through a shoal of white water which had the consistency of concrete at times. "Any more brilliant remarks from you and I'll write a letter to the postmaster general complaining about his cheap help."

"If you don't get those crackers back here pretty damn fast, the mailman won't be bringing you a paycheck at the end of the month," Greg called to her over the noise of the engines, showing that his temper hadn't improved.

"You heard the man," Jeff taunted her. "Besides, you'd better sit down—there's another rough patch of water coming up."

That was enough of a warning to stop the discussion immediately, and Dany scuttled carefully back to the end of the bench where Greg and Liza were ensconced, the package of graham crackers clutched in her hand. "Sorry to be so long," she said. "She might do better in your lap for a few minutes—there's some white water ahead."

"I see it." Greg settled the baby firmly in his lap, and as she opened her mouth to protest, he said quickly, "Give her something to eat—that'll help her enjoy the ride."

"Here you are, Liza," Dany said hurriedly, bringing out a cracker as a diversion.

"Not such a big piece," Greg admonished, breaking two tiny pieces off the cracker and putting one in each of Liza's hands. "This way, there's no chance of her choking. And hang on!" he told Dany as they started into the churning rapids. "Otherwise you'll be in the bilge—"

Dany gave a muffled shriek as she was jarred to the end of the bench when the *Belle* fishtailed in the strong current. She tried to grasp something solid and found herself clinging to Greg's arm to avoid an inglorious tumble onto the deck.

"Are you okay?" he wanted to know.

"Yes, of course. Oh, damn!"

"What's the matter?"

"I squeezed the crackers—they're all crumbs," she wailed, peering with dismay down at the plastic bag.

"Who cares? Sit down, for Pete's sake—until

we get through this stuff." He cast a frowning glance toward the side, where spray was slicing in as the jet boat lunged around a partially submerged rock in the middle of the channel. "I hope your chum knows what he's doing."

"They don't give them a license to run the Snake if there's any doubt." She nodded toward Jeff's intent figure at the wheel. "He had to serve an apprenticeship of 365 days with a qualified pilot before he could take his exam."

At that moment the white water eased and Jeff turned to give them a cursory glance over his shoulder. "Everything okay?" and then, "Five more minutes to the bend. Tell Liza that help's in sight."

"Very funny," Greg said, trying to settle the squirming youngster in his arms again. "She's doing her damnedest to crawl overboard."

"Here come the crackers." Dany was searching out the biggest of the broken bits and carefully deposited one in each tiny hand. Liza's eyes sparkled as she saw her prizes and shifted her attention. The bigger cracker disappeared immediately into her mouth and she watched with unswerving concentration as Dany frantically searched for a replacement.

"Take your time," Greg said. "From the looks of things, our supply will last about five minutes. Once that's gone, we're out of luck. Unless you wanted to divert her by changing her diaper again."

"I'm sure that Liza would rather wait for her mother to do it," Dany said, keeping her glance on the little girl.

"And I'm damned sure that you would," Greg observed with a chuckle.

Dany's gaze came up reluctantly to meet his and then she grinned. "At least I'd do better than last time. I couldn't do any worse." The sight of a car driving along the narrow winding road at the edge of the river to their right prompted her to add, "This is the last gasp for civilization. All the amenities like electricity and telephones stop at the Bend. It's the freight-distribution spot for Hells Canyon, too. Most supplies are trucked there and then go by boat for the next fifty miles."

Greg's eyebrows went up in surprise at her words. "It's hard to realize that there's still such isolation in this part of the country. Almost like the old maps where there were blank spaces . . ."

"Or the ones that said 'here be dragons.' At least we don't have to worry about that."

"Just our diminishing graham-cracker supply," he said, shifting Liza on his lap. "Keep them coming, will you?"

"Sorry." Dany hastily put another bit in the little girl's outstretched fingers. "There you are, sweetie."

"Is there any hope of a cup of coffee when we get up there?" Greg asked as Jeff steered the boat through the channel around some white water and they caught their first sight of some buildings clustered ahead at the edge of the river.

"Sure thing." Jeff had lowered his speed in the middle of the turn and he was able to hear Greg's question. "We'll take twenty minutes or so to deliver Liza and get pumped up with coffee and muffins."

"You mean there's a restaurant up there?" Greg asked hopefully.

"You bet. Being at the end of the road is good business. They've got a finger in everything."

"That means freight hauling and a lodge, of sorts," Dany added when Jeff turned his attention to throttling down in the current so he could bring the *Belle* alongside the pier at the Bend complex.

"Who lives in the A-frames?" Greg wanted to know, jerking his head toward the distinctive cabins beyond the big buildings and the marina.

"Employees. A few stay all year. The owners take on extra help in the summer. At least they used to," Dany said.

"They still do," Jeff confirmed, spinning the wheel to bring the boat into a vacant berth. "Looks as if we have a reception committee."

"I didn't think Liza would stay unclaimed for long," Greg said.

"Can you hold her still for a minute?" Dany asked, trying to brush the last of the gummy cracker crumbs from the baby's tiny fingers.

"From the smile on her mother's face, she won't mind," Greg said, hoisting the baby to his shoulder and giving a reassuring grin to a dark-haired woman who was practically dancing with impatience as she waited halfway up the slope by the locked pier gate.

"Why all the padlocks? That's something new, isn't it?" Dany asked.

"There's been some pilfering lately. Nothing stays the same," Jeff said noncommittally as he cut the engines and nudged the boat against the pier. A waiting man quickly slipped a bowline in place while another, older man cinched in the stern. It was all done with a minimum of effort and the two immediately turned back to loading freight on the other side of the pier.

"Apparently we're not as far from civilization as it looks," Greg said wryly, getting carefully to his feet as he still held Liza. "Do you want me to deliver this package?"

"Might as well go ahead with her," Jeff said. "I'll bring the rest of her stuff. Dany, can you manage okay?"

"I'll be fine." She gave Liza a farewell pat on the bottom and watched anxiously as Greg stepped carefully over the railing onto the pier.

"I'll wait for you up by the gate," he promised, hoisting Liza to his shoulder and starting off. "From the sound of things, she's getting hungry again."

"It was handy you two were along," Jeff acknowledged to Dany as he gathered the baby's belongings in one hand and a canvas mailbag in the other. "I wasn't looking forward to this trip with a baby in my lap."

"You would have managed somehow." Dany checked to see that she'd put her handkerchief back in her pocket. "Actually Greg did most of the work," she added reluctantly.

Jeff's grin was taunting as he stepped easily onto the pier. "That's right, he did. I hadn't planned on mentioning it. He could give you some lessons along that line."

"I'll be sure to remember." Her tone was dry. "I was going to ask if you want me to carry anything for you, but now I'm not so sure—"

"Those newspapers have to come," he cut in briskly. "Drop them off at the coffee shop. I'll meet you there."

Dany's lips curved in a rueful smile as she bent to gather the newspapers he'd indicated. She seemed to have a talent for surrounding herself with strong-minded men who treated her as if she didn't know enough to come in out of the rain. Obviously she'd have to show them they weren't going to have it all their way.

A longer glance around her showed the owners of the Bend had expanded the place tremendously since she'd visited the last time. There were two deckhands working on a small jet boat nearby and two other husky freight handlers stacking some plastic bales alongside the *Belle*. Probably animal feed for one of the ranches up-river, she thought, as she piled the last rolled newspaper in her arms and made sure that the strap of her shoulder bag was secure. From the corner of her eye she could see that Greg had handed Liza over to her mother by the gate and had turned back impatiently to see what was keeping her.

A newspaper slipped and Dany tightened her grip, muttering an annoyed, "Damn!" as she awkwardly clambered over the railing onto the pier.

Afterward she couldn't remember feeling any apprehension when she skirted the towering stack of plastic bags up by the bow of the *Belle*, but as she passed, one of the heavy bales plummeted from the pile onto her shoulder. Her newspapers cascaded onto the concrete and pain shot through her side as she was shoved forcefully against the *Belle*'s metal railing.

Even as she clawed at it to regain her balance she felt herself slipping between the boat and the pier as the hull bobbed from the wake of another jet boat which had just passed in the channel.

The hull surged toward her as Dany hung in the void between the rubber fenders and the concrete pier, trying to escape unscathed. Her fingers scraped desperately on the metal as she struggled to pull her legs up to evade the trap caused by the metal boat and the surging river—knowing sickeningly all the while that it was too little, too late.

She didn't see what propelled her upward a split second afterward when she was flung to safety over the boat's railing, but the metallic grating of the hull against the concrete pier came through the cold, clear air with horrible clarity.

Dany shuddered as she lay sprawled, unable to

move. That grinding sound could have been her death knell. She knew that fact as well as her own name and the awareness made fear cling to her body like a winding sheet and a sudden nausea rise in her throat.

4

"For God's sake, are you all right?"

The voice was familiar but there were rough
nuances which made Dany doubt her senses.
Maybe she'd lost her mind, after all. Greg Fremont had never spoken to anybody in that tone
since she'd known him. Her eyelids fluttered to
check and then they went wide with surprise
when she found his anxious face just inches away
from her own.

"Can you move?" he wanted to know, his
glance still boring into hers.

"I think so," she murmured, and then yelped
with pain as his hand hit a tender spot when it ran
quickly over her thigh. "That hurts."

"Come on—let's get you back here on a bench
and do some mopping up." His clasp was firm but
gentle as he supported her along the pier and half-
lifted her into the stern of the *Belle,* where he'd
cradled Liza such a short time before.

The work at the boat on the other side of the

pier continued without interruption; the plastic bag that had slid from the pile and knocked her off her feet still lay untended at the edge of the pier.

"If you hadn't seen me . . ." she began, and then broke off because she couldn't keep her voice steady.

"But I did and that's all you have to think about now," he said, pulling out a clean handkerchief and starting to brush away the dirt from her clothes and hands. "I'll have a word with those two a little later." He jerked his head toward the two men still loading the plastic bags on the boat at the other side of the pier. "Not that it'll do any good."

"It must have been my fault. Probably I hit the edge of the pile when I went by." Dany ran still-trembling fingers through her hair and tried to think. "I can't remember. There was the noise from that boat on the river, and I suppose it drowned out everything else. It happened so fast —all I can remember is hanging there, knowing I couldn't . . ." Her voice broke again.

"What you need is some coffee. Can you walk up the hill?" Greg's voice was briskly back to normal.

"I'm all right," Dany said, determined to match his tone. She stood up and followed him to the rail, managing to step back onto the pier with only the slightest bit of a limp. "Jeff will wonder what's happened to us. I'd rather you didn't say anything about all this," she added as they threaded their way down the narrow pier toward the hillside steps.

Greg's glance was hooded as it flicked over her. "Whatever you want," he agreed finally as they reached the gate where he'd carried the baby earlier. "Incidentally, Liza's mother sent her thanks to you."

"You should have told her that you were the strong right arm and deserved the credit."

"You were the graham-cracker repository," he said, gesturing her ahead of him toward the stairs leading up the hillside to the restaurant above. "Don't ever underestimate your worth."

"I'll remember that when I ask for a raise." It was an effort to keep her tone light because she was discovering that she ached in any number of embarrassing places and right then all she wanted to do was hobble back to the boat and nurse her bruises in private.

Greg must have been watching her closer than she thought, because his hand came under her elbow to boost her up the last flight of steps. "I refuse to discuss anything other than a cup of coffee right now. Maybe we'd better make sure to have some food to go with it if this is the last outpost."

"It might not be a bad idea. Jeff said something about a new cook up at White Water." She waited for him to hold the door and then stepped into the big room with windows along one side overlooking the river and all the activity at the pier below. Some of the tables were occupied but there weren't any waitresses in sight.

"This looks like self-service," Greg said, gesturing toward a counter with a big coffee urn on it at the end of the room. "You'd better sit down and I'll bring your coffee over." He craned his neck to see what was on the big tray alongside the urn. "Looks like muffins. How about some?"

"They sound heavenly." Dany frowned slightly as she surveyed the big open room where the other customers were obviously more interested in conversation than service. "Usually things aren't quite this casual. I wonder where Jeff's gone."

"Who knows?" Greg shrugged. "He'll turn up."

"Mmm, I suppose you're right." She noted her dirty palms with distaste. "I'll certainly have to find some soap and water before I touch anything."

"In that case, get a move on," Greg told her as he walked toward the coffee bar. "Otherwise, I can't guarantee there'll be anything left." He hesitated long enough to give her an intent look. "Are you okay?"

Dany could feel the heat rising in her cheeks under his searching appraisal. "I'm fine," she said hurriedly. And then, when he still looked unconvinced, she said with more conviction, "Really."

When she returned to find him seated at a round table under the windows ten minutes later, she wasn't surprised to find herself still under scrutiny. Greg got to his feet to pull out her chair as she approached and then said with approval, "That's an improvement. You don't look like the resident ghost any longer."

"At least I'm a cleaner one. That coffee smells wonderful!" she said, sitting down and beaming as she saw a plate with hot blueberry muffins in the center of the table. "If those are half as good as they look—"

"They are. I sampled one while I was waiting for you." He pushed a saucer with butter pats and a knife toward her. "It was almost worth getting up at the crack of dawn for this."

"Hells Canyon isn't the easiest place to make connections," she admitted, buttering a piece of muffin after taking a satisfying sip of coffee. "And it gets worse from here on. You're sure that Miss Logan has things arranged for her trip?"

"You don't have to worry about Sylvia." Greg's tone was complacent as he helped himself to more coffee from a carafe he'd brought to the table. "She's really efficient no matter what she tackles. An amazing woman."

"How nice." Just as if Sylvia were a rare commodity considering her sex, Dany thought as she tried to get her words out without choking. Greg hadn't said that his missing Sylvia wouldn't fall into streams or hang on the edge of a jet boat like a wimp from *The Perils of Pauline*, but the accusation lurked underneath. She took a deep breath and tried again. "Have you known her long?" she asked, keeping her glance carefully lowered.

Greg had turned his attention to the middle of the river, where a rafting party was trying to maneuver through some white water so they could beach their big rubber craft just beyond the pier. "I don't think they're going to make it," he murmured.

"Then they'll have to row awhile and be a little late for breakfast." Dany waited for a moment and tried again. "I asked if you've known her long."

"Known who?"

"Sylvia. Miss Logan. Your accountant," Dany said through tight lips. "You shared an airplane with her." And God knows what else, she thought irritably.

"Oh, Sylvia." Once the rafters got out their oars, Greg lost interest and turned back to his coffee. "We grew up in the same neighborhood." He obviously didn't want to dwell on the subject because he shot a frowning glance at his watch. "Where in the devil is that mailman of yours?"

"Jeff? He's not my . . ." Catching Greg's annoyed look, Dany broke off to say, "I don't know. I can't imagine. He's pretty friendly with most of the people here." She pushed back her chair and got to her feet. "I'll go look in the kitchen. They probably have a new blond waitress and Jeff's trying to rearrange her social life."

"I've heard about rain and sleet and hail . . ."

"Well, as far as Jeff's concerned, a blond waitress has more clout than the weather. They're his weakness . . ." Dany broke off as the restaurant's outer door flew open with a bang and she beheld Jeff standing there with a woman she didn't recognize. "I take it back," she said slowly. "Apparently he's just discovered brunettes. I must say, he has good taste." Her words came to a halt again—this time when the startlingly attractive young woman by Jeff's side caught sight of Greg.

She flung out her arms and came toward him at a dead run. "Darling! How's this for a surprise!"

Dany stepped back so she wouldn't be trampled when the brunette threw her arms around Greg's neck, and barely heard his strangled "Sylvia!" before the young woman in his arms gave him an enthusiastic kiss.

Greg called it quits first and he looked slightly disconcerted as he pushed the girl back to arm's length an instant later.

"Sweetie, I haven't embarrassed you, have I?" The woman in his clasp brushed a careless hand through her gamine haircut. "It's so good to see you again."

"How the devil did you get here so fast?"

"I'll tell you as soon as I have some coffee," the girl said, and then turned her bright gaze on Dany. "I'm Sylvia Logan. You must be—"

"Dany Livingstone," Jeff cut in behind them. "And no more than five minutes for that coffee,

Miss Logan. We're way behind schedule already. I'll be down at the *Belle* getting things aboard," he added to Dany and Greg. "Remember, you two, five minutes. No more."

"We'll be there," Greg promised. "Even if Sylvia has to carry her coffee with her."

"Don't be like that, darling." Sylvia had poured some coffee from the carafe and was using the mug like a hand warmer between her palms. "I've been coming nonstop for hours."

Greg gestured for Dany to sit down again and subsided into his own chair as he said, "Okay, let's have a capsule version of how you got here."

"Well, after you left Morgan Brothers they found out that they couldn't decide on how to handle their equipment amortization schedule, so they're going to send the information to Chicago next week. I tried to get the plane you were on but finally had to settle for a charter. I knew I'd be too late to catch you at the marina, but at the airport they told me I could hire a car and meet you halfway. How's that for an extra effort?" Her eyes widened soulfully. "Besides, I knew it would be a lot less expensive than hiring another jet boat for the trip upriver."

Greg's sudden grin took years from his face. "That's my girl. Underneath that glamorous exterior, a frugal female."

"Absolutely the best money can buy," Sylvia said, meeting his smile with one of her own.

Dany scrunched down in her chair, suddenly feeling as welcome as Dracula at the blood bank.

She'd had plenty of time to survey the newest arrival and, even without her near-miss with the river, she wouldn't have held a candle to Sylvia Logan's elegant appearance. A metallic pewter-colored trench coat provided a remarkable foil for her dark hair and eyes. The upstanding collar framed a white turtleneck cashmere sweater which was both practical and good-looking. On her feet she wore a pair of high-heeled black Italian leather boots which flattered her long legs. Aside from her clothes sense and striking figure, she was pretty enough to have every man in the room staring at her.

"Have you had enough?"

As Greg's question penetrated, Dany blinked, realizing she didn't have the foggiest idea what he meant. "I . . . I beg your pardon."

"I wondered if you're ready to go." He turned to Sylvia, adding, "Miss Livingstone had an accident down on the pier just after we arrived."

As if she still only had one oar in the water, Dany thought, furious at his careful tone.

"Do I have to call you Miss Livingstone, too?" Sylvia asked Dany, looking like an exotic bird with her head cocked to one side as she stared across the table.

"I hope not. My name's Danielle. Dany most of the time."

"Good," Sylvia said briskly. "I'm Sylvia." She glanced at the man by her side expectantly.

"It probably makes more sense to skip formality from here on," Greg said, getting to his feet after a casual appraisal of the pier below. "Jeff must be ready for us—he's just standing around talking down there. You two go on ahead."

"I hope he put my things aboard," Sylvia said, allowing a slight frown to mar her smooth forehead. "He promised he would when he picked me up. I'd better check, though."

Dany slipped her purse on her shoulder and started toward the door with her. Greg calmly went to pay the check at the cashier's desk in the corner of the room, where an older woman had materialized.

"Where did Jeff find you?" Dany asked Sylvia as they left the restaurant and headed for the path down to the river.

"In the parking lot." The brunette turned an amused gaze her way. "He'd just finished saying farewell to a blond who was driving back to town."

"The blond waitress," Dany murmured.

"She could have been—I didn't ask. Jeff came over to help me with my bags and introduced himself after I mentioned Greg's name." Her expression was thoughtful as she observed their river pilot's lanky figure on the pier. "They grow them big in this part of the country. Have you known him long?"

"Long enough. To be taken sparingly, or the result can be disastrous."

Sylvia's carefully tended brows rose slightly. "That's how I had it figured. All the interesting ones are that way, aren't they?"

A gurgle of laughter rose in Dany's throat. She managed to subdue it and say solemnly, " 'Fraid so," as if she had a thick diary of memoirs to back her up.

"I'm glad we're not walking upriver if this is as fast as you can go," Greg said, approaching from behind. He shepherded them onto the pier and kept a casual hand at Dany's elbow as they walked down to the *Belle.* "Everything ready?" he asked Jeff as they reached the bow of the jet boat.

"All set." Jeff tossed a careless salute to an older man on the boat at the other side of the pier who was loading the last of the plastic bags. Dany gave the stack plenty of room as Greg helped her over the railing, and she subsided thankfully on a metal seat at the stern. She noticed two elegant pieces of luggage by the wheel, which Jeff was shoving into the covered storage forward. Then Sylvia was aboard and Greg was standing by the stern line. The older man on the other boat ambled across to let go of the bowline as Jeff straightened behind the wheel and started the engines.

"Something tells me I'll need this." Sylvia was pulling a silk scarf from her pocket to cover her black hair as she settled on the bench beside Dany.

"There's less breeze forward if you'd rather," Dany told her. "The bench beside Jeff is the best."

"Is this one of those buses where you can't talk to the driver?" Sylvia asked.

Dany had to lean forward as the roar of the jet engines increased. " 'Talk' isn't quite the right word."

Sylvia nodded. "I get it. Screaming time. Will he let me steer?"

"Not if I have anything to say about it," Greg said, coming over beside them after coiling the stern line.

"Darling, don't you be so stuffy," Sylvia said, patting his arm possessively as she got up. "Oh, help!" she yelped, clinging to the end of the seat when Jeff accelerated and headed for the channel in the center of the river.

"If you're going to move around—hang on," Greg warned, putting a steadying arm at her waist. "It gets a lot rougher than this."

Sylvia clutched her scarf, which had already slipped off her head. "You've convinced me. Right now, I think you need seat belts on this thing."

"She'll be better up forward," Dany told Greg when he frowned.

"What about you?"

"I don't mind the breeze. It smells good after all the months of big-city air."

"And the spray?" he asked, still lingering.

"Most of my clothes are plastic or washable."

"Look—this is no time for a convention," Jeff called over his shoulder. "There's a stop at a ranch in about five minutes, and after that, no moving around."

"You heard him, Sylvia," Greg said, urging her carefully forward to the bench seat which was protected by a windshield and a plastic side curtain.

"But I wanted to learn something about Hells Canyon," Dany heard her say when Greg turned and started toward the stern again.

"Ask Jeff. All I know is that it's Idaho on one side and Washington on the other, with the Snake River underneath." Greg ducked as a sheet of spray came over the edge when Jeff made an abrupt turn to stay in the marked channel. "And I sincerely hope to heaven that it stays there," he said in Dany's ear as he slid onto the end of the bench beside her.

"What stays where?"

"The Snake." His forehead creased as he stared over the rail at the surging gray water cascading past them when the *Belle* labored against the current. "Right now this river looks like the Atlantic. You didn't tell me that we were going to set out in a peapod."

She grinned. "Wait'll we pass some kayakers—then the *Belle* looks like a cruise ship. Besides, there's some wonderful scenery up the way a bit."

"That remark sounded positively maternal." He laid his hand carelessly over hers in her lap. "Do we cling together if the going gets really rough?"

Her pulse leapt but she managed to keep a

straight face. "You don't have to worry. Jeff has transported all ages and hasn't lost a passenger yet. Except for one or two who got seasick," she added as the craft fishtailed in the current.

"Now she tells me."

"You're not regretting those muffins?" she asked, wondering suddenly if he could be serious.

"Only that I didn't have the last one on the plate." He glanced down to rub her fingers. "Didn't you bring any gloves?"

She looked blank. "I honestly don't remember." Then, as he started to chuckle, "What's funny about that?"

"I was just thinking how different you are from Sylvia." He nodded toward the wheelhouse, where the brunette was engaged in an earnest conversation with Jeff. As she pointed to something on shore, Dany could see that she was wearing a pair of black pigskin gloves. Obviously the woman packed as she did everything else—with efficient thoroughness.

"I'd let you borrow mine—"

Greg's casual comment brought her back to reality in a hurry. "That's not necessary, thanks—" she began, only to have him interrupt as if she hadn't spoken.

"—except that I forgot to bring mine, too. You didn't mention how cold it gets here."

"I don't remember any discussions on the weather."

"We must have held one." He was watching the scenery beside the river with concentration—just as if he'd never seen a rocky gray hillside before. "And I should know. That's all we've talked about since you started to work for me. There've been a few lapses about freeway snarl-ups, but the weather is obviously your true love."

"I didn't know that I'd bored you," Dany said, pulling her hand abruptly out of his.

"The hell you didn't. Don't try to convince me that you're in a mental straitjacket with anybody else. Your friend Jeff, for instance," he said, jerking his head toward the pilot's broad back.

"That's ridiculous. I've known Jeff for years . . ."

"Well, we're not overnight acquaintances by now either, but I'm not getting anywhere!" His glance went down to her hands, which she'd tucked up her jacket sleeves to try to keep warm.

Dany blushed under his wry gaze, but before she could reply, Jeff had cut the power and was navigating the *Belle* carefully over to the right-hand shore, where an oil drum rested on its side atop a stone cairn. A rough path led up the sloping hillside behind it, and in the distance the roofline of an A-frame structure could be seen, as well as some farm outbuildings.

"Dany, come up here and do some legwork," Jeff said with a quick look over his shoulder. "That way, I won't have to tie up. It's that bundle of papers and the long package for the Martins," he added, gesturing toward the mail he'd stored forward.

"Don't bother Dany—let me," Sylvia told him, already scrabbling for the things he'd indicated.

"Not with those heels," Jeff said, stopping her as she straightened with the package. "If you didn't break your neck on that gravel, you'd sure as heck scratch the paint on my boat."

"I would not—"

Greg cut into her heated reply as he stood up and said, "I'll do it. Where do I put the stuff—just shove it in the oil can?"

"I am perfectly capable of handling it," Dany cut in, annoyed at the way Greg was taking over for her again.

"You may be capable, but that's no reason for you to have all the fun," he said, keeping a firm hand on her shoulder. He waited until Jeff nudged the bow into the soft shoreline and then took the bundles from Sylvia and made his way to the bow. With his long legs, it was easy for him to drop down onto the gravel beach, avoiding the surging water around the hull. He put the mail into the oil drum, even using a piece of plastic which he found in the makeshift mailbox to carefully wrap the protruding end of the package and protect it from the weather.

"Anything to pick up?" Jeff called as Greg hurried down the slope.

Greg shook his head and vaulted over the mailboat rail, lingering at the bow just long enough to fix a line which had come uncoiled.

"Right. Hang on." Jeff waited until he was

alongside the wheelhouse and then put the powerful jets in reverse and, an instant later, the *Belle* was again on her way upstream.

Dany's lips were still tight with annoyance as Greg slid onto the edge of the seat again. "Relax," he said, seeing her stiff profile. "You're going to be aching in every bone as it is, after what happened at the Bend. There's no sense in getting more bruises playing postman just because you want to show me how efficient you can be."

"I wasn't trying to do anything of the kind," she said weakly, not really surprised to find herself on the defensive again. It was beginning to feel like home territory.

"That's good, because I already know," he said, folding his arms over his chest.

He looked about as immovable as the fifty-ton bronze Buddha at Kamakura, Dany decided, sneaking another sideways glance. And his expression wasn't a mirror of kindness and benevolence either. However, she *did* ache in more places than she cared to think about, and it was nice of him to remember. Probably the least she could do was acknowledge it. "Thank you," she said after a considerable pause.

"You're welcome," he replied after a matching one.

She kept her attention on the shoreline from then on, but the silence that settled between them wasn't uncomfortable. After a few minutes she relaxed and forgot about trying to stay dignified in her delight at being on familiar ground again.

Each mile upstream saw the canyon walls getting steeper as the ranches spreading out on either side of the lower Snake disappeared, replaced by a few vacation homes perched along the water's side or the occasional fishing lodge with two or three jet boats bobbing at the dock.

The rocky hills wore a sparse covering of brown grass, evidence that the summer had been hot and dry as usual. Small scruffy trees made a token showing in the deep draws, but their twisted trunks proved that only the strong survived in the rough terrain and severe climate. Even the broad river itself was a formidable brownish-gray color—hardly the bubbling clear current of so many Western waterways.

A surge of that gray water came over the side as Jeff increased speed through still another rapid, and Dany ducked to avoid the spray. She collided with Greg's shoulder before he pulled them both out of range with a quick reflex action that was even faster than hers.

"Sorry," Dany said, sitting upright again and brushing off the water that clung to her sleeve.

"No problem. You'd better stay close. It looks as if we've got a run of white water." He gave her a narrowed glance. "But then, you know more about that than I do."

"There's quite a stretch of it here. Oh, there's the Runyan place." She gestured toward the shore ahead of them to the left, where the rooflines of two or three weathered structures could be seen past the rocks at the river's edge. "I wonder if . . ." she began, and then she started to smile as Jeff cut the force of the engines and maneuvered out of the channel.

"How about brunch?" he asked, glancing over his shoulder. "I never did have a decent coffee break this morning."

When he turned back, taking their acceptance for granted, Dany started to laugh.

"Now what?" Greg asked.

"Jeff may be the mailman, but he's done this run so many times that he can't resist acting like a tour guide, too."

"It just looks like a deserted farm to me," Greg replied in an undertone. "Not that I'm against stopping for a few calories. There's something about this fresh air . . ."

"Greg, darling, isn't this fabulous?" Sylvia asked, standing to face them as Jeff expertly throttled up to a break along the rocky shore, which obviously had been used as a jet-boat moorage before. "You didn't tell me it would all be such fun."

"Wait until she finds that the plumbing is nonexistent," Dany muttered. "This place has been abandoned for years."

"You can be the one to mention that," Greg replied as he got to his feet, then saying in a loud tone to Jeff, "Want me to fasten that line onto a rock or something?"

"I'd appreciate it. Hang on while I nose her into the sand," Jeff instructed. "Now—get off and tie the line around that tree snag by the rock. It usually works fine. Dany, you'd better show Sylvia the path and watch that she doesn't turn an ankle in those boots."

"The way you go on, anybody would think you had a footwear fetish," Sylvia flared, spots of anger showing on her elegant cheekbones.

"Not on your life. I just don't want to take time to run you back down to the nearest doctor after you fall on your face. And before you get off, take a thermos of coffee," he told her while Greg was fixing the line ashore.

Sylvia's chin went up and she shot Jeff an annoyed look. "I can't possibly manage to carry your coffee *and* watch out for potholes in the path too. Besides, it's your job to carry the supplies on this boat, isn't it?" She scrambled over the side of the *Belle* and made her way up to where Greg waited on the shore.

"Somebody should have warned you," Dany told Jeff with a smile, "smart men don't give orders these days."

"Silly twit," Jeff muttered, cutting the engine and putting the key carefully in his shirt pocket. "Who in the hell does she think she is?"

"Just a paying customer."

"Tell your stepfather that. I'm not impressed. Are you above carrying a thermos of coffee?"

"Not if that's the only way I'll get a cup," Dany

replied calmly as she bent to pick up a nylon pack with two flasks and some plastic cups. "I didn't think I'd be hungry again so soon."

"You'd better eat while you have the chance. I'm not too sure about your stepfather's new cook at the lodge. She may need a while to settle in."

"I thought you said she was highly recommended."

"That's what Evan told me. Of course, you know how he goes on . . ."

"I certainly do." There was acid in Dany's words, which she made no attempt to hide. "Is she good-looking?"

Jeff shrugged as he straightened with the box of lunch in his arms. "Not bad. If you like faded blonds on the hefty side. She must have been a dish about twenty years ago."

"Then I imagine that Evan wrote her references himself. Does he still fancy himself as the upriver Casanova?"

Jeff's reply was abruptly interrupted by Greg's terse "What's holding things up?" from where he stood by the bow.

"Not a thing. Just organizing my packhorse here," Jeff replied glibly. "You go on, Dany."

"I'll take the stuff," Greg said, reaching for it when she came to the bow rail. "Is there anything else for me to carry?"

"Jeff has the rest." Dany's gaze was searching the overgrown shore as she came lightly down on the gravel, taking care to avoid the puddles of water. "Where's Sylvia?"

"She took off up that path." Greg's eyebrows came together in a sudden frown. "Is there any chance of her getting lost?"

"Not unless she digs a hole and falls in it," Jeff said, resting the lunch box on the rail while he vaulted ashore. "Your lady friend has a short fuse."

"Sylvia?" There was puzzlement in Greg's tone. "I hadn't noticed it. Usually she's pretty sensible. What did you say to her?"

"Nothing to make her go off like a rocket."

Greg frowned and then said with resignation, "I'd better see if she's all right. Are you coming?"

The last remark was directed in an absent-minded way at Dany, and after an instant's hesitation she shook her head. "I'll be along. There are some pictographs here that I want to see."

"I didn't know there was anything like that around here. I'd like to see those myself." Greg sighed before adding, "Well, maybe there'll be time later."

Jeff was checking the line on the tree snag, but he glanced up the path after Greg disappeared. "If Sylvia wants to keep him around, she'd better behave herself," he said, picking up the lunch box again. "When a man sounds more interested in pictographs than—"

"Watch it," Dany cut in.

"—than pulchritude," Jeff went on with a taunting glance, "then don't count on collecting his Social Security check."

"Greg could give you lessons in handling pulchritude. He doesn't even have to think about it. It's a natural gift—like getting taxis in the rain or a dinner reservation without subsidizing the headwaiter's Florida vacation. Are you going to bring the lunch box or am I expected to carry that as well?"

"Getting up early has soured your disposition, sweetie," Jeff said, hefting the box easily against his chest. "I'm just keeping you company while you inspect the pictographs."

Dany started up the path ahead of him, saying over her shoulder, "You know very well that was an excuse. There hasn't been anything really interesting around here since those vandals made off with that rock slab a while ago. The police didn't ever catch them, did they?"

"Nope. Not a trace." Jeff frowned at her. "How did you hear about it?"

"Evan. He mentioned it in a letter."

"I didn't think you wrote to each other."

"We're not pen pals, but there's a fair amount of estate correspondence. Right after Mother died there was a lot. These days, he just forwards reports from the lawyers." Despite her attempts to keep the conversation light, it was difficult for Dany to disguise the bitterness in her voice on the last comment.

"At least you don't have to try to get a decent

salary out of the man. His type goes all the way back to Dickens. I suspect that Scrooge paid the same hourly rate."

"I'm surprised you've stuck this long." Dany held back an overhanging branch as they climbed the steep path. Her glance went down to the swift-moving current of the river and then across the rugged canyon with its straggly patches of green between the rock walls. The surroundings could be menacing but withal there was a peace and majesty that brought a lump to her throat. Her lips crooked in a smile as she saw Jeff follow her glance, and then she said, "It doesn't make any sense to love this place. But I do, and you do too."

"Yeah—and maybe we both should see a psychiatrist. Except that I can't afford one on what your stepfather pays me." He jerked his head for her to go ahead of him on up the path. "We'll probably feel better after some food."

"Where do you want to eat?"

"Might as well use that broken foundation of the old barn for a table."

"With a convenient rock for a chair?" She flung him a rueful smile over her shoulder as the path leveled. They came out on a partial clearing where some sagging timbers and crumbling rock walls were all that remained of the old homestead. She lingered for an instant, taking in the dusty smell of the place, and felt herself going back in time. Nature had taken over since the ranchers had left; rust covered the discarded wheels on a piece of farm machinery nearby, and wildflowers bloomed by an old stone wall which was all that remained of the family's well. Insects buzzed in an overgrown shrub and a shore bird squawked as he winged from a tree beside the riverbank, announcing that he didn't approve of the intruders in his realm.

Jeff brushed past her to deposit the lunch box on the broken wall and frowned as he looked around the deserted scene. "Now, where do you suppose they've gotten to? Maybe I should go back down to the *Belle* and give a blast on the horn."

"They can't be far . . ." Dany tilted her head inquiringly as she decided that she heard the murmur of voices on the path that led from the back of the homestead to a river overlook.

"Well, go rustle them up," Jeff said unfeelingly, starting to sort out plastic-wrapped sandwiches. "They might not be hungry, but I am, and your boss has the coffee. Why in the deuce didn't he leave it here before he started a scenic tour?"

"Stop complaining," Dany said, giving him a comforting pat on the arm. "I'll go find them."

"Just bring the coffee. If they want to feast on the landscape, it's up to them."

Dany was still grinning at his caustic comment as she hurried along the other path, and then her expression froze as she rounded a corner and saw Sylvia and Greg standing close together. Or at least as close as her employer could manage, considering that he was still holding on to the nylon pack containing their coffee. As Dany stood stricken, uncertain whether to interrupt them or disappear discreetly, Sylvia's arms tightened and she pulled Greg's head down to give him a quick kiss.

Dany winced visibly and then tried to retreat— to go anywhere so that she wouldn't have to see Greg take over the initiative in that embrace. Unfortunately, in her hurry to get away, she stumbled over a rock on the path, blundering into a bush an instant later.

She must have sounded like a battle of the Trojan War, because immediately she heard Sylvia saying, "Dany, for heaven's sake—are you all right?" and a moment afterward Greg's steadying hand on her elbow.

"I am perfectly fine," she snapped, shaking it off. "Jeff sent me along to say that lunch is ready —whenever you are."

"I'll bet that his invitation wasn't half so diplomatic," Sylvia said, tossing her head. "It doesn't matter. I'm starved. Are you coming, Greg?"

"Right behind you," he assured her, but put out an arm to detain Dany when she would have followed. "Hold on a minute." His voice was authoritative as he stared intently down at her. "Are you sure you're still functioning?"

"Of course I am. What makes you think that I'm not?"

"Well, this certainly isn't your day. I'm beginning to think you're accident-prone."

"Just because I fell off a dock?"

"And now into the shrubbery. To say nothing of taking a header into a Montana creek."

"I'd prefer that you would," she advised him stiffly.

"Would what?"

"Say nothing more about it. Besides, you're hardly in a position to talk."

"What's that supposed to mean?"

"That shade of lipstick you're wearing doesn't do much for you," she told him, her words coming out like ice chips.

His dark eyebrows climbed, but if she'd been hoping to embarrass him, it didn't work. He merely hauled a handkerchief from his pocket and handed it to her.

"What's this for?" she asked.

"To get rid of the lipstick—naturally." His glance dared her to object, and after weighing the alternatives, she shrugged, scrubbing the corner of his mouth where traces of Sylvia's enthusiastic kiss remained.

"All neat and clean," she said finally, handing the handkerchief back.

His lips twitched as he pocketed it. "The perfect secretary. And so happy in her work."

"Should I write a memo advising her to switch to a more permanent brand in the future?" Dany asked, matching his tone.

"Certainly not. This way I get the best of both worlds. Did you say something about lunch?"

Dany flounced angrily ahead of him back down

the path, trying to ignore his chuckle behind her. Damn the man! Every time she crossed swords with him, she came out bleeding.

As if by mutual consent, the conversation over lunch kept to the commonplace. Sylvia perched on an end of the crumbling fence while she consumed a roast-beef sandwich, balancing her coffee as if she'd been eating in the midst of deserted homesteads all her life. Jeff, who'd clearly not forgotten her imperious air at the beginning of the picnic, thawed visibly as the meal progressed. Greg was seemingly content to sit atop a nearby stump and enjoy the sunshine as he ate. Dany eyed him warily, wondering if his air of idleness were genuine or assumed for the occasion. He made no reference to their recent skirmish, nor were there any languishing glances toward Sylvia. Either that romantic interlude didn't rank with the apple turnover he was con-suming or he was doing an excellent job of camouflaging his emotions.

When Sylvia had finished her coffee and neatly placed the plastic cup in the garbage bag for transport back to the boat, she looked around with an expectant air. "Now I want the deluxe tour," she told Jeff. "There must be a fascinating history to this place. Do you have time to show me around?"

"There's not all that much to see anymore . . ." he began, as if he suspected her olive branch might be poison ivy.

"Nonsense. What about the people who lived

here? Why did they leave? And you said something about Indian pictographs."

"The best ones are gone now. There are some more upriver we can see from the boat."

"Aren't there any left around here?" Sylvia asked, getting to her feet.

"Well, yes. But it's a hike up the path behind what's left of the barn over there," he said, jerking his head in that general direction.

"I'm ready to go." She turned to Greg. "Want to come?"

To Dany's surprise, he shook his head. "Not this time. There are some things I want to find out about White Water Lodge before we arrive on the scene, and this is a good time to learn. Unless, of course," he said to Dany, as if the idea had just occurred to him, "you feel the need for some exercise."

It would have served him right if she'd announced she was palpitating to stride through the weeds to look at the mediocre pictographs which were all that remained at the farm; but she decided to be sensible. "Not right now. I've just gotten comfortable on this rock."

Jeff shot her a resigned look which showed what he thought of her excuse, and then got reluctantly to his feet. "Okay, we'll go," he told Sylvia, gesturing toward the overgrown path. "Watch where you're walking. You're too heavy for me to carry very far." He watched Sylvia march off ahead of him, her chin high, before he turned and winked at Dany. "This may be a short tour," he announced.

Dany found Greg coming across to fill her coffee cup again when the other two disappeared up the path. After that, he topped his own, wedging the thermos against the wall before settling down beside her. Another sideways glance showed that he was staring at his coffee with unnecessary concentration. She took a deep breath and said, "You don't have to worry about Sylvia. Jeff's completely reliable—"

"I never worry about Sylvia," he cut in. "She can take care of herself. I only hope that Jeff can."

Dany stared back at him, hoping that she didn't look as confused as she felt. Then her lips tightened. It was one more prime example of the man's callousness toward women. She'd had him pegged right at the beginning.

" . . . you could straighten me out on a few things."

Greg's voice penetrated and she jerked back to the present, wondering what he was talking about.

"I want to find out about this stepfather of yours," he repeated, spelling it out so that she couldn't possibly misunderstand. "What's the background on this lodge property? Does he have a legal right to handle the sale?"

"Oh, yes." Dany looked down at her coffee, her tone flat and unrevealing. "He's the executor of my mother's will. She hoped he'd share the proceeds if he felt it was necessary to sell the lodge, but he isn't legally bound to."

"Then the property . . ."

"Came from my mother's family. She ran the lodge after my father died, but she wasn't the businesswoman type. Evan originally came along on one of the jet-boat tours to spend two weeks with us. He works at charming everything in skirts and he's had a lifetime of practice," Dany added, pouring the remainder of her coffee onto a sparse patch of grass which was struggling to survive. "I went east after college, and the next thing I heard, they were married."

"Were they happy?" Greg might have been asking about the price of potatoes for all the emotion in his voice, and Dany was grateful for his cool facade. If he'd murmured any words of sympathy, she probably would have burst into tears or some other silly thing.

As it was, she managed to shrug and say, "Who knows? Evan wears a thousand faces. He probably managed to say the right thing until my mother became ill. Afterward, when he stuck her in the hospital and forgot to come around very often—no, she wasn't happy but she was too weak to cope. We didn't discuss the property or legal matters then. There were more important things to talk about."

"I'm surprised that you've come back here on a vacation," Greg said after a pause.

"I wanted to collect the rest of my belongings

that I'd stored at the lodge." She put the empty cup on the ground by her knee. Looking up, she encountered Greg's steady glance. "I wonder why Evan called you in on this."

"Maybe he didn't know anyone else—or he thought we'd work a little harder, since you were connected with the firm."

"That's ridiculous," she sputtered.

"*Isn't* it," he agreed in a bland tone that made her grind her teeth.

"You know what I mean . . ."

"It isn't hard to figure out," he said in a "lay-it-on-the-line" tone that she'd heard before. "But your stepfather probably thought he was covering all the bases. It would help shut you up, for one thing—in case you had thoughts about seeing a lawyer to protect your interests. No court could fault his actions, when the other heir was in it from the beginning." He paused for a minute, as if undecided how to phrase his next words, and then went on carefully. "Of course, that might be taking too much for granted. Will your stepfather do anything to look after your interests when it comes to the sale of the property?"

She shook her head. "Of course not. Morally, he's supposed to . . ."

"But?"

"Evan Monroe has all the morals of a tomcat."

"Then this trip can't be very pleasant for you." He gave her a searching look. "Am I right?"

She shook her head slowly. "I'm numb to all of

it by now. Even my stepfather can't change the fact that this was once home. There are still a million memories beyond his touch." She got to her feet and gave Greg a crooked smile. "Evan will be quite charming, so you needn't worry about getting in the middle of a family feud."

Greg stood up beside her, his frown showing that her disclaimer hadn't convinced him. "Maybe—but it's still a mess. I wish I'd known— I wouldn't have touched this project with a barge pole."

"Don't feel that way—actually I'm glad you're here." She started to laugh as she confessed, "And you can't be any more amazed than I am at hearing that."

His hand covered hers to give it a reassuring squeeze. "There are still a few miracles around, after all. At least now I don't have to worry about your tipping me out of the boat while we're going upriver."

She flushed and took a step backward as Sylvia's light laugh could be heard from the path nearby. "I just hope that the two of you won't be too bored while you're at the lodge. It was always on the primitive side, and I can't think Evan has done any maintenance since he's taken over."

Greg smiled slightly, his own gaze on Sylvia and Jeff as they approached, obviously in a better frame of mind than when they'd left. "It looks as if Sylvia's adapting just fine. Jeff must be a more persuasive tour guide than I thought."

"He can be nice, but you don't need to worry. He's seldom serious for long," was all that Dany could say to reassure him before the others came again on the scene.

"I hope you aren't hankering to see any more of this place," Jeff said to Greg as he bent to stuff the remnants of their lunch back in the box. "Sylvia can give you a thumbnail sketch on the way upriver if you don't mind. We'd better get going now or Evan will be out on the dock with a shotgun."

"And from what Jeff says, your stepfather isn't a man to be trifled with," Sylvia said to Dany.

It was apparent that she wasn't seriously worried about the prospect, because her cheeks were flushed and her gaze lingered on Jeff's tall form, watching him police the picnic area in a few deft motions. He finally gave the place a satisfied look and ushered Dany and Sylvia toward the path to the river, saying to Greg, "You'll bring the thermos?" and giving a satisfied nod when the other looped the nylon pack over one shoulder.

"Then we're off," Jeff said briskly. "I hope everybody had enough to eat, because that's it until we get to the lodge."

"And how far is that?" Sylvia said, looking back at him.

"About forty-five minutes—watch where you're walking! I told you those heels were a menace." He strode up beside her where she was waggling her ankle experimentally after stumbling over a rock in the overgrown path. "Are you okay?"

"Yes. Sorry. I'll be careful."

Sylvia's meek reply was a far cry from her demeanor before lunch, Dany decided. But the question was, how had he achieved it? Jeff's tour must have worked another minor miracle. She slid a sideways glance toward Greg to see how he was taking Sylvia's new attitude, and discovered him inspecting a stone with some faded Indian pictographs.

"Not the best of specimens," he muttered, apparently intent on Indian history for the moment.

"No." Dany felt the least she could do was keep his attention diverted from the other two. "The good slab is gone. It was pilfered one night years ago and is probably sitting in some collector's backyard right now."

"Are you back on that old story?" Jeff said, sounding annoyed. "I need some help to cast off when you two are ready."

Greg's brows came together but his voice was calm when he replied, "Sure thing. Climb on board and I'll shove off when you give the word."

The *Belle* was launched again without any difficulty. Jeff was back in good humor again when Greg pulled himself aboard and made his way along the rail by the wheelhouse.

"Didn't get your feet wet, did you?" Jeff asked

as he turned the *Belle* from reverse out into the mainstream of the river.

"Not enough to bother," Greg replied. "If there's any more mail to be delivered, I'm your man."

"I think I could make a convert out of you," Jeff told him. "Too bad we don't have a full load of tourists. They manage a good round of applause on the difficult deliveries."

"*Is* there any more mail to be delivered?" Dany called, raising her voice over the noise from the jet engines as he accelerated.

"Not today. Sit back and relax. White Water Lodge is the next port of call."

Greg's gaze took in Jeff's set jaw after his announcement, and Dany's tense figure. He bent toward her, saying, "I can understand why you aren't enchanted at seeing your stepfather again, but damned if I can figure out why Jeff looks as if he's on his way to the guillotine."

"I'm not sure myself." Dany chewed on her bottom lip as she stared at Jeff by the wheel. His expression had lightened slightly as he bent to answer a question of Sylvia's, but Greg was right: he wasn't the carefree companion she'd known on earlier visits.

At that moment, the river channel narrowed and the canyon walls seemed to tower over the *Belle* when Jeff took the very middle of the channel in a series of rapid "steps." White water pounded the bottom of the hull and the boat turned and slid in the currents like a live thing, as they managed to evade the rocks. By the time they'd passed through that particular rapid, Greg evidently had second thoughts.

"I take it back," he said, leaning against Dany for an instant. "If I had to go up and downriver in this cement mixer every day, I'd look grim too."

"You're probably right. Although it doesn't seem to have dampened Sylvia's spirits," Dany said. Despite the spray and the wind, the brunette was obviously having the time of her life.

Greg's reply didn't do anything to raise her morale. He shrugged and said, "I never have to be concerned about Sylvia."

From his tone, Dany knew that he'd caught the drift of her thoughts, because there was amusement underlying the words. She kept her gaze straight ahead as she said, "Good—then I won't worry about it." Pointing toward the left side of the bank, she added crisply, "That river coming in ahead of us is the Salmon. It attracts a lot of rafters and white-water addicts in season. Probably you've heard about it."

After that, she kept the conversation strictly on the scenery as the *Belle* continued to hurtle up the Snake. She dutifully drew his attention to deer on a promontory and even two mountain goats perching precariously on a steep hillside. Sylvia had unearthed her camera by then and insisted on Jeff holding the boat in place despite the swift current while she tried for a picture.

"Another piece of film wasted," she said cheerfully when Jeff insisted on getting under way. "But they were so beautiful I just had to try." She bent impulsively to drop a kiss on Greg's cheek as she squeezed past him. "I'm *so* glad that you invited me to come on this job."

Dany wilted against the rail as she watched. She could see why Greg liked Sylvia—to be truthful, she was having a terrible time trying to hate her herself, despite having every reason to.

By then, every jar of the boat was making her wince. The tension rose as she recognized her surroundings and realized that White Water Lodge was just around the curve of the river.

When she caught her first glimpse of the familiar scene and saw her stepfather's figure on the pier, she knew that the nagging beginning of a headache she'd felt for the last five minutes wasn't going away. If anything, it would get considerably worse.

5

Greg's silence beside her made her realize that White Water's outward appearance hadn't brought him to his feet cheering. The lodge itself, with its peeled-log exterior and wide porch overlooking the river, fitted neatly onto the gently sloping hillside, and the lawn surrounding the cottages was a bright green, evidence that Jeff or someone had been watering during the hot days. But even to her frankly sentimental glance, the string of cottages looked tired and run-down, with missing shakes on the roofs, sagging porch railings, and rusty lawn chairs at the doors. Whatever Evan had been doing with the estate funds, it wasn't maintenance of the resort.

Even Sylvia's face registered dismay, although she smiled gamely when she caught Dany's glance. "At least the place doesn't look crowded," she announced to Jeff when he throttled back to maneuver to the pier.

"Didn't Dany tell you? You and Greg are the only guests," he said, keeping his attention on the bow of the boat and ignoring the waved greeting of the man on the dock.

Dany would have liked to do the same thing but knew there wasn't any point in it. She had made a mental resolve that she'd stay polite during her stay at White Water despite any of Evan's controversial comments. There was nothing, however, that required her to make her stay longer than absolutely necessary. "A quick in and a quick out," she murmured, managing to smile as she returned her stepfather's wave.

"What did you say?" Greg asked.

"I was repeating Rothschild's motto for investing in the stock market," she said, keeping her tone light.

"Only it wasn't the stock market that was on your mind, was it?" His glance went quickly over the resort's boundaries and she knew that he hadn't missed anything on the way. "There's considerable acreage in addition, I understand."

"That's right." She nodded toward the hillside behind the lodge. "It's over there. Grazing land mostly. There's quite a river frontage as well."

"The land will be what sells the place," he told her, not bothering to soften his pronouncement. His mouth was stern as he went on. "This all belonged to your mother's family?"

"That's right." Her voice was equally terse.

"It seems a damned shame . . ."

"Now that I don't have any family left, I find that it really doesn't matter all that much." As Jeff cut the engines and moved swiftly to toss a line to the man on the pier, she walked over to the railing of the *Belle* and said, "Hello, Evan—it's been a while."

The gray-haired man straightened after looping the line around a bollard on the pier and came back to help her over the railing. "Dany, my dear —it's been far too long," he said in deep fruity tones, pulling her to him with a bearlike hug. His kiss landed on her ear as she turned her head, ostensibly to introduce the others.

"Evan, this is Sylvia Logan . . ." She waited while Sylvia was ushered ceremoniously onto the pier and then added, "Greg Fremont."

Evan Monroe's affectionate guise changed and he shook hands in a businesslike manner when Greg came onto the dock. Her stepfather was the shorter of the two, but there was nothing of the "casual rancher" in his appearance. His wool slacks were immaculately tailored and blended with the houndstooth check of his cashmere sport coat. Dany noted that he'd gained weight since she'd last seen him, giving him a suggestion of a double chin, but his graying hair was still thick and his skin smoothly tanned. Nothing there to make her dislike him, and she knew that he could be charm itself when the occasion demanded. Unfortunately, the charm disappeared quickly when there was no need to impress the audience, and underneath, there was vindictiveness and a temper which flicked his victims like the tip of a leather whip. She watched him bending solicitously over Sylvia and decided that the temper would be carefully cloaked on this trip.

"I'm sure that Dany will do the honors . . ." Evan was looking at her inquiringly.

"Sorry." She pulled herself back to the present with an effort.

"I was just saying, my dear, that I'll need Jeff to take me back downriver. You won't mind escorting Greg and Miss Logan—or may I make it Sylvia?"

"Please do."

Sylvia had gravitated to Greg's side and become a demure employee within seconds of landing. Dany's lips twitched; Evan wasn't the only person on the dock playing a role.

"Jeff and I will try to get back as early as possible," he was saying then. "The only trouble is that I may have to go all the way to the Bend before I can complete my business." Turning to Greg, he added, "Unfortunately, that will hold up our discussion. I should think that Danielle could show you around in the meantime. She knows almost as much about the place as I do—even though she hasn't been back to visit as often as I'd hoped."

All he needed was a violin playing "Hearts and Flowers" in the background, Dany thought, keeping a smile on her face with an effort. It was needling that was typical of Evan, and he was waiting expectantly for her sharp reaction. She took a deep breath and managed to keep her voice unperturbed. "I'll be glad to help Mr. Fremont if I can."

Her stepfather's eyebrows went up. "I know you work for him, but surely it isn't necessary to be so formal here on the river."

"My feelings exactly," Greg assured him. "But don't worry about us. You go ahead with your business downstream."

"I'll have to unload some cargo. There's food to be refrigerated, and the bags . . ." Jeff began, obviously unhappy at the prospect of another jaunt on the river so soon.

"I can take care of it," Greg said, going back to the boat to help him. "From the looks of things, I won't have much else to do."

"Do go ahead, Evan," Dany urged, knowing she'd be in a better mood as soon as he was out of sight.

"But you haven't met Hazel." Her stepfather's genial air was wearing a little thin as he started to lose control of the situation.

"Where is she?" Dany wanted to know.

"Up at the lodge, of course. . . ."

"Well, then, we'll introduce ourselves," Greg said easily. "She *is* expecting us, I hope."

"So do I," Dany said fervently. "It would be a real catastrophe if we insulted Evan's brand-new cook."

"She's really more than just a cook," Evan said quickly, and then caught himself. "I think she could handle some managerial duties if we were here for another season. She's a very competent woman. If this property deal weren't so important, I'd go back up to the lodge with you." He took time to bestow an annoyed look on Jeff. "Actually I thought you'd be here long before this."

"That's my fault, I'm afraid," Sylvia announced. "I wanted to inspect that abandoned farm where we stopped to eat, and Jeff was kind enough to humor me."

"I see." Evan made a visible effort to do a little humoring himself as he recovered his jovial expression. "I can't blame Jeff a bit for taking advantage of the opportunity. When I come back, you must let me show you around the property here—but in the meantime . . ."

As if he'd snapped his fingers, Jeff finished his offloading of stores and got behind the wheel again. "Would you handle the lines, Greg," he called as Evan maneuvered himself over the rail and sat down in the seat that Sylvia had occupied earlier.

"Sure thing." Greg had a thoughtful look as he started toward the bowline again, lingering by the wheelhouse just long enough to ask, "Want to take what's left of the coffee with you?"

"No, thanks. I'll scrounge a cup later at the Bend if we have to go that far." He watched Greg free the lines, gave a thumbs-up gesture to the women who were watching, and the *Belle* set off with a roar downriver.

"My God, he doesn't waste any time when he's going with the current, does he?" Greg commented as they watched the boat disappear around the bend of the river in no time at all.

"I hope he knows where those rocks are," Sylvia said, standing at his elbow with a worried look on her face. "One mistake and he could rip out the bottom of that boat. . . ."

Dany chuckled and shook her head. "I'll have to tell Jeff that you two were standing here writing his obituary. Why do you think they make river pilots serve that year's apprenticeship?"

Greg shook his head ruefully as he reached for two of their bags. "I just hope that he makes a hell of a lot of money. He certainly earns it!"

"I agree with you on that. Wait a minute, Sylvia," Dany said when she saw the girl reach for a box of groceries. "We don't have to work so hard. If things haven't changed, there's a jeep by the lodge and we can get most of these stores in one trip."

Greg promptly dropped the bags back onto the dock. "That's the best news I've heard all day. Let's go meet the redoubtable Hazel and see if she has the car keys hanging alongside the dinner menu."

Dany would have led the way up the rutted track except that she found her arm taken by Greg, while he managed the same courtesy for Sylvia on his other side.

"Who's pushing who up this hill?" Sylvia said with a giggle. "It looks to me as if Dany and I are expected to do all the work."

"I told you she was smart," Greg complained to Dany. "I can't get away with anything."

"Not much, you can't," Sylvia teased, reaching up to ruffle his hair.

Dany kept her lips in a determined smile, aware that every move the two of them made showed a long time intimacy. It was strange that she hadn't heard about Sylvia before this. But then, Greg wasn't the type to parade any serious affections for all to see. Probably the dates she'd heard about while she'd worked for him were simply window dressing—and camouflage window dressing, at that.

Sylvia stopped halfway up the steep track to get her breath and observe the river running so strongly below them. "You know, I was just wondering what you do up here at night," she said to Dany.

"You spend a lot of time praying that the generator keeps working. Otherwise it's back to candles and heating water on the stove—a gas stove."

"That isn't what's bothering me," Greg said, shoving his hands in his pockets as he surveyed the lodge and the cottages beyond. "How about an emergency? What happens when Jeff isn't here with the boat to go for help?"

"That's the serpent in Eden," Dany confessed, meeting his gaze honestly. "Fortunately, most of the year-rounders have a two-way radio these days. It's the only way that parents with young children will agree to the isolation. They've heard too many horror stories when there wasn't emergency medical help here in the canyon. Now, generally, they can summon a helicopter from Lewiston if weather permits."

"What about nighttime?" Greg wanted to know.

She simply shook her head.

"Then we'll walk carefully and I'll make sure that you don't take a header into the drink down there," he said with a slow grin.

"I think I've exhausted my quota of disasters for this trip."

"My God, I hope so—for the next two or three, as well."

"What in the world are you two talking about?" Sylvia wanted to know.

"Family joke," Greg said, and gave them both a gentle shove up the track. "Come on. We'd better make an appearance at the lodge or Hazel will think there's nobody around for dinner."

When they reached the deck of the lodge a few minutes later, a woman opened the door, showing that they needn't have worried about being unobserved.

"I'm Hazel Lowery," she said. "Welcome to White Water Lodge."

Dany's eyes widened at her "chatelaine-of-the-castle" manner. Evidently Evan's new cook had been reading up on aristocracy, because the blond turned and motioned them inside with a regal gesture. The only thing she missed was, "I now proclaim this cattle show open."

Even Greg stood uncertainly waiting for somebody to go first, and his sudden frown made Dany suspect that he was already regretting the planned stay. She saw him rub his chin before saying, "I'm Greg Fremont," in a courteous tone. And then, "Sylvia Logan, who works with me." His hand came back to pull Dany to his side. "Of course, Mr. Monroe has told you about Dany."

Hazel's eyes went dismissingly over Dany's wrinkled clothes and windblown hair before she said, "Of course. He's been anxious to see you again. If there's anything you need to make your stay comfortable, please let me know."

She wouldn't have had to use her imagination to figure out what to do, Dany decided. There were some basic suggestions like, "Sit down and I'll heat some coffee," or "Let me show you to your rooms." But no one made a move, and the woman stayed posed against the big leather sofa.

She must have been unaware of the incongruous picture that she presented in her fuchsia dress trimmed with a mammoth ruffle which outlined the low neckline. Since her middle-aged figure was of Rubenesque proportions, the brightly colored outfit would have caused a second glance anywhere; among the Early American furnishings of the lodge the contrast was mind-boggling. And if the dress and high-heeled sandals weren't enough, there was suspiciously blond hair pulled up in an intricate style and rouge dusted generously on her cheeks. Her background scene should have featured bead curtains, gilt bird cages, and possibly a leaning lamppost, Dany thought, trying to keep her expression suitably bland. That part was important, she knew, because even the heavy cosmetics didn't hide Hazel's shrewd pale-blue-eyed glance.

It wasn't hard to figure out why Evan had been attracted to the housekeeper, and Dany suspected that Hazel's talents didn't center around a kitchen range.

That speculation became a certainty when Greg cocked his head and said, "I smell gas. Are you having trouble with the stove?"

Hazel's lips clamped in an irritable line. "Evan says it's the heater. I thought he shut it off before he left. I suppose I'd better check."

Greg nodded. "I certainly would. I'm surprised you didn't notice it earlier."

"My sense of smell isn't all that good." She waved a casual hand toward the furniture. "If you want to sit down, I won't be long. Then I can allot your rooms."

Greg waited until she'd disappeared down the long hall which separated the big open kitchen area and the public part of the lodge. "Are there any bedrooms in here?" he asked Dany.

"One combination study and master bedroom. Then there's a smaller guestroom. If that hasn't been changed too." She went over and raised a window close to the fireplace, sniffing with relief at the sudden draft of air.

"Thank heavens," Sylvia said, coming over beside her. "Hazel . . . er . . . what's-her-name . . .

must not have any nose at all if she can't smell the gas in here."

"She may not have much of a nose but she sure as hell has an abundance of everything else," Greg commented, opening the door to help the fresh air circulate.

"That may be, but I'm still surprised that Mr. Monroe went off and left her in charge," Sylvia said.

"I'm not," he said with some amusement after a careful glance down the empty hallway. "She doesn't miss much. Evan doesn't need to stick around. After all, why bark if you have a dog?"

Dany's lips twitched. "I think you're right. Besides, he doesn't have to worry about my getting away with the family silver. He took the only boat."

"Is that the only way out of here?" Sylvia wanted to know.

"For all practical purposes. There's the jeep— but it's thirty miles over a horrible dirt track before you reach a decent road, and then another twenty until there are any bright lights."

Sylvia bit her lip and gave Dany a sympathetic glance. "And you grew up here?"

Dany smiled. "There were compensations then."

The sound of a door slamming at the end of the hallway made Greg straighten and say, "I might as well get our stuff off the dock. Is it okay to take the jeep?"

Hazel heard the last part of his question as she

came back down the hall, replying before Dany had a chance. "I brought the keys with me," she said, dangling them from fuchsia-tinted nails. "I thought you might need them."

"Thanks very much." There was a dry undertone to Greg's voice. "Do you want the supplies brought up, too?"

"Why, yes." Obviously it hadn't occurred to her that there was any question about it. "Evan told Jeff to bring some steaks. I certainly hope he managed to buy decent ones this time."

Greg hovered on the threshold. "How about the gas leak? Did you take care of it?"

The narrowing of Hazel's glance showed what she thought about his abrupt tone. "Naturally. Otherwise I would have mentioned it first thing."

So that sharp blue-eyed glance wasn't misleading, Dany decided. No matter how much the housekeeper draped herself over the furniture and played the "helpless woman," she apparently had a major role in the running of the lodge.

Greg went to bring up the supplies and Hazel drifted over to the window until she was satisfied that he wasn't going to run the jeep off the road into the river. Then she turned to survey Dany and Sylvia, saying languidly, "There's instant coffee if you want to make some, and cookies if Jeff filled my order properly."

"I'd hate to spoil dinner," Sylvia said, looking at her watch. "I think I'll pass on the coffee, thanks."

Dany stayed perched on the end of the sofa.

"What time did you plan to serve dinner?" she asked Hazel, keeping her tone casual.

"Around seven, I think. The steaks can be cooked outside on the barbecue. One of you girls might enjoy making a tossed salad to go with it." She bestowed a complacent smile on both of them. "It's more fun if we share the tasks."

Dany's intuition told her that Hazel's idea of sharing wasn't going to be restricted to food. "How about our rooms?" she asked bluntly. "If the generator is as temperamental as it used to be, we'd better get unpacked before dark, too."

Hazel nodded approvingly. "And it gets dark early here in the canyon. Once Greg comes back with the food, I'll tell you about your quarters."

The jeep could be heard laboring up the hill on the return trip, and as Hazel went over to the door to supervise its unloading, Sylvia sidled up to Dany to murmur, "Maybe after dinner we can all gather round the campfire for community singing."

"Only if you and I mimeograph the song sheets," Dany said.

"I was sure that Greg said we were paying for our rooms."

"You probably are. That wouldn't make any difference to my stepfather or Hazel," Dany said with a grin. "At least I've figured out why he hired her."

"Besides her measurements?"

"Uh-huh. Evan was always partial to overripe and sexy widows in the tour parties, but it isn't that." She paused as the housekeeper reappeared in the doorway, beckoning to them. "We're coming, Hazel."

"Don't leave me hanging," Sylvia hissed as she followed Dany toward the door. "What's her fatal fascination?"

"She could step on a dime and tell whether it's heads or tails. Even wearing those fuchsia-colored sandals."

"And your stepfather?"

"He would appreciate it. Although Evan's dimes would never slip through his fingers to fall on the ground in the first place. Now I'll go wash out my mouth with soap," she said in normal tones as they came up to the jeep, where Hazel was checking the items against a list.

"You'll have to check the hot water first," the housekeeper said absently. "There wasn't much left after I finished my bath."

"I beg your pardon . . ." Dany said, bewildered.

"I said," the older woman went on with elaborate patience, "that you'd better not wash anything until I check the hot water supply. I think everything's here, Greg," she went on, folding the list and putting it in the box. "Now, if you'll take the perishables into the kitchen—I'm sure the girls will help you carry the rest of the things," she added over her shoulder as she marched back to prop open the screen door. Afterward, she stood in the middle of the room and with graceful gestures indicated where to put the supplies and gave a sigh of satisfaction when they'd finished. "Now, I suppose you'd like to see your rooms before the cocktail hour. I've already prepared our snacks for that."

"It wasn't necessary for you to—" Dany's protest stopped abruptly when Greg applied a warning pressure to her elbow.

She glanced up, puzzled, but he was smiling at Hazel as he said, "That sounds good. Maybe you can clue me in so I can get started with the appraisal even if Evan's late getting back."

"That shouldn't be any problem. He has the previous financial statements ready for you. Although if Evan can come to terms with this deal he's working on . . ." She paused, her expression smug.

" . . . I'm out of a job," Greg concluded pleasantly. "At least I've had a chance to see the famous Hells Canyon." He turned a bland face to Dany. "Are you going to lead me to my cottage?"

Hazel cut in before Dany could reply. "I'm afraid that it's going to be a little inconvenient for you—especially tomorrow night when Evan's back. Tonight, one of you can have his room here in the lodge."

"That won't be necessary—" Dany began, only to be cut off again when Hazel continued.

" . . . because there are only two cottages ready for guests. Evan had the rest painted just before I came, and they haven't completely dried. I'm sorry about it, but at least two of them have been aired today and it shouldn't be too bad sleeping in them. And there are two beds in each one," she concluded brightly, "so you can work things out however you like."

Dany cringed inwardly, remembering the gracious hospitality that once had been dispensed at the lodge. She took a deep breath and said to Sylvia, "You have Evan's room to-night—if that's all right." Too late she remembered that embrace she'd interrupted at the homestead and shot an uncertain glance at Greg. Maybe he would have preferred Sylvia within easy reach at the cottage. His next words made her feel better.

"That sounds like a good idea. You could use some rest after playing catch-up on the airplane to get here," he told Sylvia. "Tomorrow I'll start cracking the whip."

"Whatever you say," Sylvia replied. "I'll come out and help get my stuff out of the jeep."

Dany waited until they'd gone out the door before she said to Hazel, "Would you like me to do anything special?"

The housekeeper's penciled eyebrows rose. "Nothing other than seeing to the beds. There should be linen in the storage room."

At least Hazel didn't expect her to do the laundry first, Dany thought with inner amusement. Aloud she said, "Right. I'll take care of it. Which cottages are we to use?"

"One and two. I thought you'd like the buildings closest to the lodge," Hazel informed her.

Dany could have told her that it would have

made more sense to select two cottages closest to the community bath facilities, which were at the far end of the property, but she managed to hold her tongue again. Sylvia could use the lodge amenities and Greg would probably take this newest inconvenience with his usual aplomb.

When he came back in the lodge carrying Sylvia's luggage, Dany let Hazel take over the hostess role and show the master bedroom. She noticed her own bags still in the back of the jeep and decided to leave them there while she was making up the beds. One good thing about White Water Lodge, there were no worries about petty thievery, since the only passersby were rafting parties or jet-boat operators, who had far more important things on their minds.

The stock in the linen storage room was depleted but Dany found enough sheets and cases to make up the cottage beds. It would be easier to fix the master bedroom during Hazel's cocktail soiree. Making the bed would be a legitimate excuse for her to escape what was likely to be a highly uncomfortable cocktail hour.

Her first glimpse of the nearest cottage a few minutes later made her groan inwardly. The small room looked like the "before" part of a remodeling project without any "after" to make it all worthwhile. There were two mismatched iron beds whose mattresses had seen far better days. Chintz curtains hung at the high windows, but there was just enough material to provide the necessary bit of privacy. Two thin rag rugs were in front of the beds atop worn linoleum which covered the rest of the small room. The only other amenities were two folded blankets and a pillow for each bed. Dany, who knew how cold the canyon could get at night, decided on moonlight requisitioning if necessary. She shook her head as she dumped the linen in her arms onto a vinyl-covered chair which was fraying at the seams. It was a wonder that any tourist would consent to stay at the lodge under such circumstances, and she would have bet her bottom dollar that none of them made a return reservation.

"Ah, Miss Livingstone, I presume," Greg said from the front porch of the cottage.

"*Must* you?" Dany was relieved to find an outlet for her ill temper. "That's a very old, very tired joke."

"At least it fits the locale. I don't know where Stanley and Livingstone finally got together, but the place couldn't have been much more dismal than this." Greg gave the interior of the cabin an irritated look as he put down the two bags he'd carried from the jeep.

"One of those is mine," Dany pointed out with acerbity.

"Two bags—two beds," he said, moving the bed linen to test the cushion of the chair and then settling into it gingerly.

"There are also two cottages. Or had you forgotten what Hazel said?"

"I wish I could." By sliding his long legs out in front of him, taking up a good quarter of the floor space in the process, he was able to rest his head against the back of the chair. "Right now, every syllable is etched in my memory. Since she repeats herself every five minutes, it's not surprising."

Dany couldn't quarrel with him on that. "I only hope she can cook," she muttered, intent on pulling two sheets out without dislodging the towels in the pile at the same time.

"Don't count on it. Fortunately, most anybody can put a steak on a barbecue."

With his hands crossed over his chest, it was obvious that Greg didn't plan on helping her make the bed. It wouldn't have hurt him, Dany thought rebelliously, and shook out the sheet with unnecessary vigor over the sagging mattress on the bed under the window. "Can you?" she snapped, giving him a brooding glance over her shoulder.

"Can I what?"

"Put a steak on the barbecue." She concentrated on making a hospital corner. "What do you think I meant?"

"With you, I'm never too sure, so it's safer to ask. For all I knew," he added casually, "you could have been talking about beds and how to make them."

"I can't imagine how you'd get that idea," Dany said, making a production out of smoothing the sheet, which wasn't easy, considering the uneven mattress.

"Well, you certainly wouldn't be talking about

sleeping in them. Not my prim Miss Livingstone," he drawled. "Are you sure that you wouldn't be more comfortable sharing these premises?"

"Very sure."

"For example," he went on as if she hadn't said a word, "we could start with just sharing the room. Then, in an hour or so, we might do a little better. On the other hand," he said with a thoughtful glance at the blankets she was shaking out atop the sheets, "maybe it's not such a good idea, after all. Are those the only covers?"

Dany's eyes glinted. Revenge might not be ladylike, but it was the best thing she had right then. "That's it," she said cheerfully. "What you see is what you have."

"No heater?"

"Hardly—except for that." She gestured toward the light bulb which dangled from the ceiling in the center of the room. "And that goes out when Hazel turns off the generator."

"My God, I didn't know I was going to take part in the winning of the West. Where did your stepfather park the covered wagons?"

"Knowing Evan, he probably sold them to the missionaries." Her lips twitched. "I take it that your proposition no longer applies? Or was it an invitation?"

Her air of satisfaction didn't go unnoticed. Greg's eyes narrowed thoughtfully. "Oh, it's still on. Only now it's a 'BYOB' party."

"Bring your own bottle?" She stared at him, perplexed.

"Not bottle. Blankets. The more the better. It's an open invitation."

"That'll be the day," Dany said. She swept up the linen for the other cottage. "I'll be back for my bag. If that won't disturb you," she managed, stepping over his feet.

"You've disturbed me before this," he said softly. "I'll look forward to it."

But when she'd finished making the bed in the adjoining cottage, she found her belongings neatly piled on the porch. It should have made her happy to avoid another confrontation; instead it was somehow disappointing to find that Greg had abandoned his flirtatious overtures so easily.

It was obvious that Hazel would be dressed to the nines for the cocktail hour, so Dany compromised by changing into a pair of beige silk slacks with a sweater of the same background color featuring a design of pale blues and greens. There were long sleeves to provide a little warmth; enough to compensate for all the cold air that the deep V neckline allowed to seep in.

When she reached the lodge, she saw Sylvia in a well-fitting black jersey dress softened by several strings of pearls while Greg had merely changed to another solid-color sport shirt, which he wore under a tweed sport coat. Hazel still looked like an alumna from the boardwalk in her fuchsia number, but she carefully arranged a white shawl around her shoulders when she went out on the deck to check the coals on the barbecue.

Dany looked over the two platters of cheese and crackers and wondered if that would be the most appetizing part of the dinner.

Like so many people who are loath to do any actual work, Hazel had definite ideas on how she wanted things done. Greg was put in charge of the steaks; Sylvia was charged with setting the table and fixing coffee, while Dany was instructed on the right ingredients for the green salad. Once Hazel approved the result, she deigned to find a bottle of salad dressing in the cupboard.

It was bland—Dany discovered that when she poured it over the lettuce. And a few minutes later, she decided that the dressing matched the rest of the dinner. Greg and Sylvia were painfully polite when Hazel held forth at great length about her life before coming to White Water Lodge. From her accounts, she was a star of the musical-comedy circuit "before television came along and spoiled everything." She didn't mention what she'd been doing when Evan spirited her upriver and, from Greg's expression, he had no intention of asking. The only time his glazed look changed to a frown was when Hazel mentioned that the lodge's two-way radio was out of commission.

"You mean that we're completely cut off up here?" he asked.

Hazel reached for her gin and tonic to take a sip

before saying petulantly, "Now that it's dark we are. Of course, while there's daylight we could fly a distress flag or stand down on the pier and hail one of the boats going by." She gave him a sharp look that was completely out of character with her "gracious-lodge-hostess" role. "I don't know why you're worried. Jeff will be able to get the radio working again. All he needs is some time and a spare part. You can check with him tomorrow."

"I'll do that," Greg said, turning his attention back to his steak.

"In the meantime, the worst that can happen is that somebody could fall out of bed," Hazel said. She picked up her fork and toyed with a piece of tomato from the salad. "Not that anything like that would happen tonight. Evan has some stories that would curl your hair about goings-on during the conventions he's booked here. But probably that's old hat to you." Her glance rested expectantly on Dany, who had decided she wasn't very hungry after all, and was cradling a coffee mug between her palms.

Hazel's innuendo made Dany want to dump the coffee over the housekeeper's pouter-pigeon bosom, but she kept her voice level. "This was a working ranch most of the time when I lived here. Later, we booked family parties or fishermen." She got to her feet before Hazel could comment on how times had changed. "Since I'm finished with dinner, I'll go make Sylvia's bed now. If you'll excuse me . . ."

"You don't have to bother with that," Sylvia said quickly. "I would have done it before this, but—"

"I know—I didn't bring the linen down," Dany admitted with a smile. "My brain's been rusting away since I arrived."

"I really haven't been here long enough to stock the lodge linen cupboard," Hazel cut in defensively. "Evan had other things he wanted me to do—more important things than house-keeping tasks. I think you have to get your priorities right in life."

As she paused to let that sink in, Dany agreed calmly, "Of course. Anyhow, it won't take me a minute. I'll be back in time to help with the dishes."

And *that* should placate the woman, she thought as she moved quickly up the hallway to the combination study and master bedroom. She turned on the light and then hesitated for a moment on the threshold, remembering those earlier, happier days at the lodge when her parents were both living. Outwardly the room hadn't changed; there were books surrounding a fireplace along one wall, her father's big desk was still at the far side of the room along with the rust-colored leather chair. There were Navajo throw rugs on the pegged floor, and the towering mahogany bedstead with one of her grandmother's patchwork quilts as a spread. The overhead light flickered then and brought her back to the present. She'd better get a move on—probably the generator was in the same run-down shape as the radio, and she had no desire to make the bed by lantern light.

Once she'd stripped Evan's sheets, she decided to store them in the closet until she could take them out to the laundry in the morning. The cedar closet was bulging with his clothes and she finally had to push aside some boxes on the floor to make room for the bundle of sheets and cases. In doing so, she discovered a red satin nightgown hanging on a hook at the very back. The scent of Hazel's distinctive perfume wafted toward her when she shoved the nightgown behind the clothing again. Evidently the housekeeper had moved out hastily. Either that, or she'd left the gown there as proof of her position at the lodge.

The woman needn't have bothered, Dany thought as she turned back into the room again. She could have told her that Evan's actions had ceased to matter as soon as her mother died. All that she wanted now was to put a considerable distance between them and make sure it stayed that way!

Sylvia arrived when she was putting a clean case on the last pillow. "You didn't have to come and help," Dany said. "This is no trouble at all."

"I'd rather scrub floors than make conversation with that woman any longer," Sylvia muttered, checking that the door was tightly closed.

"Watch it," Dany cautioned softly. She gestured toward a grille near the baseboard.

"That opens onto the hallway. Supposedly for heat, but . . ."

Sylvia pursed her lips thoughtfully. "I see what you mean. It's all right, though. Hazel's still in the midst of telling Greg about her career behind the footlights, and she has at least fifteen years yet to go."

"Musical comedy, wasn't it?"

"So she claims. I'd guess that she was third from the left in a bump-and-grind burlesque show. Either your stepfather's eyesight is failing or Hazel knows where a body is buried in the closet."

Dany was tempted to mention that the only body in the closet would be garbed in red satin, but thought better of it.

"Greg would like to have deserted too," Sylvia went on, "except that he didn't have an excuse. He gave me a filthy look when I left him alone in there." She giggled as she thought about it, and sat down on the edge of the bed when Dany had plumped the pillows finally in place.

"I've always found that our employer manages to extract himself from sticky situations without much trouble," Dany said. "I hope you'll be comfortable."

"Well, the mattress is good," Sylvia said, giving an experimental bounce. "I feel a little guilty—making off with the best room in the place while you two are out in the boondocks. At least the air is fresher out there."

Dany nodded, because whiffs of gas fumes still

lingered in the lodge even though the defective heater was turned off and Hazel had made a token effort toward airing out the main rooms. "The ventilation isn't great in here," Dany admitted. "That's because Evan boarded up the windows to save on heat in one of his mad moments. You can't even open the damper in the fireplace unless somebody's cleaned the chimney lately."

"Oh, I'll be fine," Sylvia assured her. "Hazel said something about a cold spell predicted for this week. Are you sure that you'll manage all right out in that cottage? I didn't see a heater in Greg's when I was there."

Dany kept her glance averted as she went over to clear a corner of the desk so that Sylvia would have a place for her things. Evidently Greg hadn't suffered any pangs of isolation after she'd left him. It was a darned good thing she hadn't dropped back by to see how he was faring, since White Water Lodge cottages weren't equipped with Do Not Disturb signs.

"I'm sure we won't suffer despite the weather. There must be lots of blankets around," she said, hoping she sounded emphatic. Unfortunately they hadn't been in the linen room when she'd toured through. The prospect of early frosts hadn't occurred to her then, but Sylvia's pronouncement was disconcerting. Frostbite was all she needed to make the day complete.

There was still more to come, because at that moment Greg opened the bedroom door to demand, "How much longer is all this going to take?"

Dany stared at him. "All what?" she asked, confused.

"Whatever you're doing in here."

"I was just getting the room ready for Sylvia . . ."

"Well, you must be finished by now. C'mon, let's get going. I'm ready for bed."

Dany's mouth dropped open but she managed to say, "I don't really understand what that has to do with me," even as Sylvia smothered a giggle from the other side of the room.

"Well, our hostess"—Greg put a scathing emphasis on the last two words—"is all set to turn off the generator for the night. I've persuaded her to wait for another ten minutes or so until we get settled outdoors. At least it'll save us stumbling along the path with flashlights."

"But why is she turning it off so early?" Dany wanted to know.

"Apparently it's been malfunctioning like the radio. Evan left orders to turn it off right after dinner."

Sylvia went over to open her suitcase. "In that case, would you two mind leaving so that I can get ready for bed? Flipping around the room by candlelight has never been my scene, and . . ." She stopped, a horrified look on her face. "My Lord, that means there won't be any hot water in the morning."

"This is ridiculous. I'll go tell her . . ." Dany

began, only to have Greg shake his head and put a forceful hand between her shoulder blades to shove her into the hall.

"There's no changing that woman's mind."

"Ssh—she'll hear you," Dany said, pulling to a halt.

"No, she won't. She's disappeared into her bedroom. . . ."

"Then me for the bath," Sylvia said, grabbing up her toiletry case and making her way around them in the hall. " 'Night, you two. I'm sorry to desert you, Greg . . ."

That time it wasn't a shove Dany received, but a definite slap on the derriere that made her gasp. "Will you get moving, woman," Greg said irritably. "My God, I don't want to still be around here when Hazel comes floating out in a purple negligee."

Dany obligingly walked down the hall, smothering her annoyance long enough to say, "Not purple—it would be red satin." She paused when they reached the open kitchen section to stare at the dinner dishes stacked haphazardly next to the sink. "Oh, Lord, what about those?"

"The dishes? What about them?" Greg had marched over to an end table to pick up two serviceable-looking flashlights.

"Well, they should be done. . . ."

"Tell Hazel about it in the morning." He checked the switch on each flashlight before opening the door. "If you can get a word in edgeways. I made the mistake of trying to change the subject on her and that's why she went off in a huff. What happened to the porch light?" he asked as they stepped outside and he closed the door behind them. "This is like falling into the dark hole of Calcutta."

"Evan persists in going back to the Dark Ages —regularly." Dany switched on her light and directed the beam down toward the path. "At least, it isn't far to the cottages," she said, trying to be cheerful about it and ignoring the fact that the long walk to the bathhouse was still to come.

They made their way carefully down the path to the first row of cottages, which were in inky darkness, since it hadn't occurred to them to leave a porch light burning earlier. When they pulled up in front of Dany's, Greg waited for her to open the door and then flashed his light onto the string which dangled from the bulb in the center of the ceiling.

"I'm not sure whether that's a blessing or not," he said when she pulled it and the light revealed the stark interior of the room. "It's surprising to me that your stepfather doesn't provide hair shirts and a bed of nails for the package tours."

"When you try that mattress in your cottage, you might think you'd be better off with the nails," Dany said, trying to sound calm, although she was finding it difficult when her employer was taking up so much of her tiny room. "Evan must have sold all the decent furnishings—these are like something out of death row."

"Not from what I've seen on television. The

prisoners toss out the warden for abusing civil liberties these days. Oh, well, there's always that old motto about 'As the night is—so shall your strength be.' "

"I think you've mangled it, but I know what you mean."

"Mmmm." Greg's frown came back as he surveyed her tired features and pale face. "You must be aching from all those bruises by now. Is there anything . . . ?"

"No, I don't need any help." Dany took a step backward, knowing that if he even reached out to touch her in her exhausted state she'd fall on his neck like a piece of wet laundry. "Thank you," she added when she finally looked up to encounter his vexed glance.

"I was merely going to suggest that you might try a hot shower before going to bed to get rid of some of the aches and pains."

"I'm sorry . . ."

"And stop apologizing!"

His last order sent her careful resolve flying. "I'm not apologizing! At least not in the way it sounds."

"Then that makes two of us . . ." At that moment, the overhead light went out as Hazel chose to enforce her bedtime decree. "Oh, for God's sake," Greg said, "this is worse than being in the army. Have you got your flashlight?"

Dany switched it on for an answer and watched him reach up and pull the string on the overhead bulb. "Waste not, want not," he said bitterly.

"You were saying something when you were interrupted," Dany said, loath to have a perfectly good quarrel diverted, since it was a way to keep him around for a little longer rather than having to endure the long nighttime alone.

The prospect didn't appear to daunt Greg, because he shrugged and started toward the door. "It wasn't important. Besides, I'm working on trying to forget things tonight. This place's bad enough in the daylight, but this way . . ." He let his flashlight beam play momentarily over the narrow bed and the windowsill, where a cold breeze was billowing the faded length of curtain. "No way," he said bitterly. "G'night."

Dany nodded and then realized it was a futile gesture, too, because Greg had disappeared into the darkness. She watched the beam of his flashlight lead him toward his cottage and then closed the door of her own quickly—so that she couldn't give in to her sudden ridiculous urge to call him back.

But when she heard the force with which he slammed his door an instant later, she knew it was a good thing she hadn't weakened. There was no doubt that he wasn't in the mood for company. And even if he had been, she would have been near the bottom of his invitation list—with only Hazel and the red satin nightgown below her.

6

It was the sound of the iron triangle which finally made her surface the next morning. Pale sunlight was pouring through the small cottage windows and she groaned as a glimpse of her travel clock showed that she'd slept far later than she'd intended. The sound of the triangle meant that breakfast was ready to be served but unless she planned to join the ranks of the great unwashed and appear in pajamas, she'd never make it.

For an instant, she seriously considered simply turning over and going back to sleep but definite hunger pangs surfaced to make her think again. After that thin meal the night before, she felt a need for a platter of bacon and eggs or mounds of pancakes swimming in maple syrup. That vision prompted her to swing her legs out of bed and reach for her robe.

She almost fell flat when she stood up. After hours weighed down by every cover and coat in the cottage, her muscles had stiffened and given up the ghost. A hot shower would be the only thing to get her moving as far as the lodge.

She reached for a clean towel and tightened the belt on her robe just before she heard a knock on her cottage door. Opening it, she discovered Greg with his knuckles poised to rap again.

He took a quick look at her tousled hair and the towel slung carelessly over her shoulder before saying, "That's what I was afraid of. You're behind schedule. Don't you want any breakfast?"

"Right now, I'd kill for a plate of bacon and eggs," she told him tersely, vividly aware of his clean flannel shirt and cotton pants, the refreshing whiff of lime after-shave, and the drops of water still clinging to his dark hair.

"Why in the devil didn't you set your alarm?" Greg wanted to know, showing that he had no intention of letting her escape as she obviously wanted to do.

"Because I didn't know that we were on a schedule," Dany replied. "We never were before." She was warming to her subject. "Who in the dickens decided to serve breakfast at a set time."

"Hazel, of course. She mentioned it last night . . ." He broke off as he saw her eyes widen, and then went on in a more apologetic tone. "Maybe you weren't in the room when she said that breakfast would be served promptly at eight."

"Maybe I wasn't. And she didn't tell me."

Greg lost some of his assurance. "Actually I think I said that I'd pass the word along," he muttered. "You'd better get dressed and I'll cover for you."

"I've got a better idea. Why don't you just go down and tell her that you forgot to mention it."

"If you insist." He didn't seem in any hurry to put her plan in action. His gaze raked her untidy figure. "How did you sleep?"

Dany started to gesture airily, until she remembered that she was clutching a handful of lingerie. "Actually, very well," she admitted, managing to drape the end of her towel over the lilac bits of nylon that diverted Greg's attention. "Probably because I had so much stuff on top of me that it was impossible to move. How was your . . . ?" She started to say "night" and then decided "bed" was safer.

"Don't ask," he said tersely, reaching up to rub the back of his neck. "Even if your stepfather doesn't complete his business downriver, I'll be early for the next boat back to town. You'd better plan to come along. I can't imagine anybody in his right mind wanting to hang around up here with him and Hazel . . ." He broke off as the sound of the iron triangle came through the still morning air again. This time there was a very determined hand behind it. "Oh, hell." Greg shoved his hands in his pockets. "I'd better get down there before she decides to close the kitchen."

"If she does, I'm going to thumb a ride from the next rafting party going by," Dany said as she brushed past him to start up the path toward the bathhouse.

Her shower was probably the fastest on record at White Water Lodge. Even so, the water was barely tepid, which showed that Hazel hadn't gotten up at dawn to turn the generator back on. As she toweled herself dry, Dany decided she couldn't blame her for that. From Hazel's point of view, all of them were a decided nuisance. At least, Evan would plumb Greg's expertise so that he'd get his money's worth out of the visit one way or another.

Dany surveyed herself in the long mirror beside the bathhouse door and ran her comb through her hair. It wasn't in the cards that she'd look elegant in jeans and a long-sleeved tartan shirt she planned to don back at the cottage, but it didn't seem as if all her sleep had accomplished any transformation. There were still dark smudges under her eyes and even the cold water hadn't brought much color to her cheeks. So she'd be pale and interesting, she told herself, and grimaced horribly at her reflection.

She pulled on a cardigan over the tartan shirt as she set out for the lodge a little later, hastily smoothing her hair again as a gust of wind swirled the dust on the path in front of her. Turning into the lodge, she hesitated just long enough to glance down at the river pier. Still no sign of Jeff or the *River Belle*. "Damn," she said softly, and made her way into the lodge.

Her first glance at Hazel showed that the

housekeeper didn't like the morning shift either. The woman wore a lemon-yellow shirtwaist and her words held the same acid quality as Dany entered the kitchen. "I'd just about given you up. I really thought Greg and Sylvia would go ahead with their breakfasts—heaven knows what the quiche will be like after sitting so long."

"Honestly, Hazel—it doesn't make the slightest bit of difference," Sylvia said, coming in from the deck just then.

"And it doesn't matter to me," Greg said as he followed her. "I need a little time to make sure that I'm awake."

"I imagine you'd like some juice," Hazel said, keeping her attention determinedly on Dany.

"No, really." Dany kept her tone pleasant with an effort as she walked over to the coffeepot and poured herself a cup. "I'm ready for anything— so bring on the quiche. And I'm terribly sorry to have been so late," she added, taking her coffee over to help the housekeeper with the serving. "It must have been the shock of breathing really fresh air again."

"Only tonight I hope that there's not quite so much of it," Sylvia said, settling down at the table nearby, where four places had been set. "I didn't bring the right clothes for this place."

"You look great to me," Greg said, giving her a cursory glance.

And he was right, Dany thought. Sylvia was wearing an elegant blouson windbreaker with bold stripes of grape and olive plus tailored pants in a matching green gabardine. She looked vibrantly alive, and the lack of amenities at the lodge hadn't any visible effect.

"I'd like to have those plates served sometime this morning," Hazel said in an ominous tone at Dany's side.

"I beg your pardon? Oh!" Dany caught sight of the quiche, which the housekeeper had dished out. "I'm sorry, I was just thinking . . ."

Hastily she put the plates around the table and then remembered to fill coffee cups while Hazel was ushered into her place next to Greg.

He surveyed the pale blob of quiche in the middle of a large white plate and said, "Well, this certainly looks good."

His slight pause before the last word made Dany's lips quiver, but she found a place at the table and added, "Mushroom quiche, isn't it, Hazel?"

"That's right. And some chicken and a few other things. A good cook doesn't tell all her secrets," she said archly as she picked up her fork.

The housekeeper didn't have to worry on that score. While the quiche hadn't improved as a result of its holding pattern in the oven, one taste of the mushroom sauce she'd poured over it showed that time wasn't solely responsible for the end result. Dany pushed a vision of bacon and eggs to the back of her mind and resolutely tackled the portion in front of her.

A sideways glance at Greg and Sylvia showed

that they were having the same difficulties, although they both uttered polite comments.

It was only when Hazel rose to her feet and offered seconds that Greg hastily pushed back his chair to proclaim that he couldn't manage another bite. Sylvia quickly picked up her own plate and took it toward the kitchen, even as she announced to Hazel that she was counting calories with a vengeance.

That only left Dany as a possible recipient. She hurriedly shoved her plate back, searching for a plausible excuse. "Actually I'm not in the habit of eating more than toast and coffee," she told Hazel, which put her in line for a lecture from the housekeeper on how a decent breakfast was the only way to start the day.

That ended when Dany offered to do the breakfast dishes as a penance for being late. Hazel accepted graciously and said that she would straighten up her room in the meantime and plan a lunch menu if she had any extra time.

Sylvia watched her sweep down the hallway and muttered, "Let's all have a moment of silent prayer that she *doesn't* have time to plan anything for lunch." She rearranged the knife and fork on her empty plate and stacked them on the counter next to the sink as Dany started filling the dishpan. "I thought Jeff and your stepfather would be back before now."

"They're not so dumb," Greg said, bringing his own plate to the counter and searching for a dish towel. "They'll arrive safely *after* breakfast." He caught sight of Dany reaching for a stack of plates on the other side of the sink. "Those are from last night," he protested.

"It's all right. You don't have to start wiping until we get to the lot from breakfast." Her good humor faded abruptly as she caught sight of some baking dishes in the oven. "Hazel must have used everything in the cupboard."

"Never mind, I'll help too," Sylvia said over her shoulder. She was investigating the bread box and looked carefully down the hallway before saying, "I think we can get away with making some toast before she comes back."

"You won't have to worry as long as I keep rattling these dishes in the sink," Dany said. "Put in a slice for me, will you?"

"Make that three," Greg said, emptying the percolator down the drain. "I'll make fresh coffee to go with it. Is there anything else in the refrigerator?"

"Some sliced cheese . . ."

"Bring it out. Bring everything out." He was measuring coffee as he spoke.

"What shall I do with the rest of this quiche?" Dany asked, frowning down at the dish in her hand.

"I think that's the first idiotic remark I've known you to make since I hired you," Greg said.

"You're right. I didn't have enough sleep last night," Dany added by way of explanation as she spooned the remainder of Hazel's concoction into the garbage. She noticed that Greg wiped dishes with casual efficiency and wasn't above handing a plate back when she hadn't scrubbed hard enough. She carefully went over the dish again and said, "Do you do windows and ovens in your spare time?"

"It depends. What kind of a deal can you offer?"

"The coffee's ready," Sylvia announced from across the room. "Shall I make the toast?"

"You bet," Greg said, dropping his dish towel over the end of the counter with a finality which showed that he had every intention of leaving it there.

"We're not finished . . ." Dany said weakly.

He put his hands on her shoulder to turn her away from the sink. "The hell we're not. Hazel can earn her salary for what's left. You didn't come up here as an unpaid skivvy—and if Evan says anything, I'll let him know that I'm the only one who tells you what to do."

"Is that coffee poured?" Sylvia asked from the table where she was buttering toast.

"It will be in thirty seconds," Greg told her, and took charge of it.

They were on their third slice of toast with cheese and second cup of coffee when they heard a blast from the river that sent Dany over to peer out the window. "It's Jeff," she said, seeing the *Belle* nosing up to the dock down below the lodge. "And Evan," she added, noticing the other figure in the wheelhouse.

"Help! That means Hazel will be back on the

scene," Sylvia said, shoving the butter hastily back in the cooler with one hand while sweeping the loaf of bread into the drawer. She barely had brushed the final crumbs from the counter when the housekeeper's high heels could be heard coming down the hallway.

"I thought you'd be finished by now," she said, stopping to peer in at the kitchen and the still-cluttered sink.

"That's what happens with cheap help," Greg said as he put his coffee mug in the sink. "Shall we go down to the dock? Maybe Jeff needs help unloading the boat."

"You three go ahead," Hazel said with a barely perceptible tightening of her lips. "I hate to have Evan see the kitchen like this."

"What do you want to bet that she'll greet him elbow-deep in the sink," Sylvia said in a heated undertone as the three of them started down the path to the dock a minute later. "She's probably put on an apron so that he'll think she hasn't been out of the kitchen all morning."

"I wish to God she'd stay out of it completely," Greg said with a disgusted look over his shoulder. "That place becomes a disaster area every time she goes near the stove. Your stepfather must have been really desperate when he brought her along."

It was hard to tell whether Greg's summing up of the situation was right or not, because Evan looked all business as he came up the path. According to Jeff, they'd left the Bend right after an early breakfast, with Evan determined to make still another turnaround after looking in at the resort.

"His potential buyer for the property promised to have an answer tonight or first thing in the morning," Jeff announced to Sylvia and Dany as they went out onto the deck of the lodge. "Evan's running credit checks with the bank, but there are some other questions on the financial side that Greg needs to answer for him."

"I love the way I'm totally ignored," Sylvia spoke up. "You may not know it, but I'm supposed to be an expert on balance sheets and figures, too."

Jeff's eyes widened as he stared down at her. "And here I was telling Evan that Greg had just brought you along for the boat ride. Lord, I'm sorry . . ."

Dany caught Sylvia's fist before it could connect with his chest. "He's just teasing you—it's his favorite occupation. I should know."

Sylvia's eyes were flashing sparks as she stared up at Jeff's unrepentant face. "Honestly, you deserve to be beaten. Don't you ever tell the truth?"

"Every other Thursday when there's a full moon. But only if I'm with a woman . . ."—he paused to choose his words carefully when he saw her eyes narrow—" . . . who's on the same wavelength. Now, can we head inside so I can sit on an upholstered chair for a few minutes before it's time to go downriver again." He rubbed the derriere of his tight-fitting jeans. "I'm getting too old for this life."

"Next he'll be telling you about his deprived childhood," Dany informed Sylvia. "You can take that with a grain of salt, too."

He turned his slow grin on both of them. "That reminds me. How was breakfast?"

"Ugh. Don't ask," Sylvia said, grimacing.

Greg appeared in the doorway, a frown on his face. "Are you spending the morning out here?" he asked, his glance lingering on Dany. "I didn't know that there was anything special to look at, apart from an overgrown vegetable patch."

"We had to stop and admire Evan's tomatoes," Jeff replied before Dany could summon an answer.

Greg's frown deepened as he surveyed the patch of withered tomato plants alongside the lodge. The recent cold nights had taken their toll and the grayed stalks hung limply, their season over.

"Evan likes anything he can tie to a stake," Jeff went on in a level tone. "It doesn't matter to him whether it's people or plants. Isn't that right, Dany?"

Greg didn't give her a chance to make more than a helpless gesture before he turned to Sylvia. "Evan wants us in his study."

"Then you won't need me?" Dany asked, knowing it was a foregone conclusion.

"I was going to suggest that you start packing

the things you want to take with you," Greg said in a way that showed he was holding on to his temper with an effort. "It's too much to hope that we can leave here today, but with any luck, we should make it tomorrow. Jeff can transport your belongings later if there isn't room in the *Belle* on one trip."

"Is he always like that?" Jeff asked Sylvia as she started to follow Greg back into the lodge.

"Sometimes he's worse. Ask Dany—she can tell you."

Jeff ignored that to say, "So you won't have any spare time before we take off downriver again?"

Sylvia shook her head regretfully. "Doesn't look like it for now. You'll be back tonight, won't you?"

"You can count on that. Even if Evan can't make it, I'll find a way," he told her.

Dany was listening wide-eyed to the exchange, and she barely let Sylvia disappear into the lodge before giving Jeff a mystified glance. "What's going on between you two?"

He turned back, obviously surprised to find that she was still there. "What do you mean?"

Her lips tightened. "Don't take that attitude with me, Jeff Coates—I've known you for too long. Sylvia isn't one of your weekend playthings. If you get out of line there, you'll have Greg *and* my dear stepfather to flay you alive."

"Greg maybe." Jeff's mouth curved slightly as

he thought about it. "Evan wouldn't give a damn. He's so wrapped up in his bank accounts that he can't see beyond the bottom line."

"I still don't think . . ."

"Oh, for Lord's sake, Dany. Stop trying for the 'Puritan of the Year' award. Sylvia's able to take care of herself."

"If she isn't, I'll help Greg push you off the dock myself."

"Where are you going?" he asked then as she turned and started toward the small outbuilding beyond the linen room.

"To pack some of my things, as Greg said. If there's any chance of getting away from this place tomorrow, I don't want to miss the boat."

The rest of the day didn't hold much to improve her spirits. Greg and Sylvia remained closeted with her stepfather in the study for the next hour or so. Then Evan came out of the lodge accompanied by a resigned-looking Jeff and they made their way down to the dock again. The slamming of the lodge door had brought Dany up from sorting some books and took her to the window of the storeroom. Standing carefully out of sight, she watched the men board the *Belle* and, moments later, saw Jeff cast off and accelerate the jet engines as he turned downstream in the fast-running current. A sudden movement out on the deck of the lodge overlooking the river made her shift her attention that way. Hazel, arms folded over her formidable chest, was watching the jet boat disappear, too, and the set expression on her face showed that she wasn't happy at being left behind.

"Oh, frabjous day!" Dany quoted softly, and turned back to get on with her sorting. It was taking longer than strictly necessary. Most of the things which Evan had piled in the room were of sentimental rather than intrinsic value. He hadn't objected to her keeping a small Victorian desk from her bedroom and her grandmother's cherry bureau, but he'd announced that naturally he would be taking possession of the rest of her mother's furniture.

Fortunately, he hadn't shown any interest in her books and other small belongings—other than to suggest that she remove them from the lodge so that they wouldn't take up space. Now that she knew how quickly he planned to dispose of the property, she could understand his impatience, but it didn't make it any easier for her to decide which items should go to her apartment and which should be donated to a local charity. Dany looked at the stacks she'd put in the "keep" category and decided she'd have to be more ruthless in her decisions or she'd need a barge and then a bank loan to get her belongings across the country.

A rumbling in her stomach sometime later made her glance at her watch and discover that lunchtime had certainly arrived. Since there hadn't been any banging on the triangle, she suspected she was the only one interested.

When she let herself into the lodge a little later,

she found the main room deserted, but there was
the murmur of voices from the study. She decided
that she'd make herself a sandwich, and if Greg
and Sylvia hadn't appeared by then, she'd knock
on the door and offer room service.

The sound of the refrigerator door opening
worked its usual magic before that was necessary. Sylvia was the first to poke her nose out in
the hallway, grinning with relief when she saw
who was in the kitchen. "C'mon, Greg," she said
in a dramatic whisper over her shoulder. "There's
nobody here."

"I'm not sure I like that description," Dany
said when they both materialized like genies at
the kitchen worktable where she was construct-
ing a ham sandwich.

"I just mean that it wasn't you-know-who,"
Sylvia said, filching a piece of ham from the
package. "How many of those are you making?"

"It'd better be three," Greg said as he moved
over to run some water in the coffeepot and put it
on the stove again. "Or maybe four. Breakfast
was a long time ago."

"And we've been working hard," Sylvia con-
curred, rummaging in the refrigerator to emerge
with a jar of pickles. "Evan is determined to
make up for lost time. He'll get his money's worth
even if we're out of here by tomorrow. That typewriter of his is in terrible shape, too."

"I could help if you'd like—" Dany began, only
to have Greg cut her off.

"There's no need," he said decisively. "Sylvia

can manage. Besides, the typing shouldn't take long once we get the figures together."

He needn't have been so abrupt in refusing her help, Dany thought rebelliously, but she kept her reply carefully bland. "If you change your mind, just let me know. Do you want lettuce on these?"

"Anything and everything."

"Fair enough. Luckily there's lots of ham." She looked up from the slice of bread she was buttering. "I suppose we'd better ask Hazel if she'd like one, too. Where is she, by the way?"

"She took to her bed. Right after Evan and Jeff left," Sylvia said in some disgust.

"Is there anything wrong? I mean really wrong?"

"She claimed she had a headache," Greg said, leaning back against the counter with his hands in his pockets after getting the coffee under way. "That can cover a multitude of sins."

"You needn't sound so cynical . . ." Dany began, and then chewed unhappily on her lower lip, wondering why in the world she was bothering to defend Evan's housekeeper.

"Exactly." Greg's tone showed that he was reading her mind again. "And I'm not cynical—just suspicious. She was surveying the dirty dishes in the sink when she was stricken."

"So for heaven's sake—don't disturb the peace," Sylvia said. "At least not until we finish lunch. She might get a bright idea about cooking something to get her strength back."

Dany held up her hands in surrender. "Okay,

I'm convinced. But I still think we should ask her if she wants a sandwich. Eventually."

"Who does the asking?" Sylvia asked craftily, and then her lips curved. "I know. We can flip a coin."

"You can flip all the coins you want, but if you think I'm going down the hall and knock on that woman's bedroom door, you're not working with a full deck," Greg announced.

"And they say it's not a man's world," Sylvia said, refusing to be squelched. "All right . . . all right . . . don't get upset," she said hastily at his warning glance. "That leaves Dany or me."

"Dany's making sandwiches," he said.

"That leaves me." Sylvia gave a theatrical sigh and put her hand to her forehead as she moved off down the hall. "All right. I'll do my best to convince her to join us."

"She wouldn't," Dany said in an appalled voice.

Greg shook his head and moved closer, to lean against the worktable. "She's having you on. Sylvia can't stand it when things are too quiet. Right now, I suspect she's a little annoyed that Jeff didn't stay around to brighten the scenery."

"He should be back tonight."

"If your stepfather decides to honor us with his presence again. He's a great one for running the show, isn't he?"

"All the time." Dany stared reflectively at the knife she was using to spread mayonnaise on the slices of bread. "He doesn't give that impression when you first meet him, but afterward . . ." She shook her head.

"Umm." There was a brief pause and then Greg said, "How are you doing with your sorting?"

"I should be finished this afternoon. My trouble is that I start reading the books instead of discarding them. And the letters . . ."

"Wrapped in red ribbon?"

She started to chuckle. "Hardly. The social life in the canyon didn't lend itself to that. Of course, it did have its moments."

"I can imagine." There was a strangely sympathetic undertone as he said, "It doesn't do to look back."

She avoided his scrutiny, her eyes suddenly glazed with tears. "That's where you're wrong. There's an old saying that it's all right to look back. You just can't stand and stare."

"See here, Dany . . ." He made an impulsive movement toward her and then stopped abruptly as they heard Sylvia's footsteps coming back down the hall. "Damn!" he said in an undertone. His voice was subdued but his glance smoldered with something that made the color flare in her cheeks. When Sylvia reentered the room, she found Dany inspecting the bread as if it were something strange and wonderful, while Greg faced the sink.

"If anybody cares—Hazel doesn't choose to leave her bed at the moment."

"That's a pity," Greg said absently, moving over to stare down at the river.

"But you can send in the dancing girls along with a sandwich," Sylvia said, turning to Dany.

"Fine." Dany struggled to pull her thoughts together and blank out that last moment with Greg. "Does she want mayonnaise?"

"Only on the sandwich," Sylvia replied. "Maybe a little mustard for the dancing girls."

"Whatever you say." Dany took a deep breath and then whirled as Sylvia's words finally penetrated.

"Welcome back to the party," Sylvia said with a broad smile.

Greg must have surfaced a little faster, because he moved over to the coffeepot to check its contents, saying to her briskly, "If you have so much excess energy, you can fix the tray for room service—and don't argue."

"Yes sir, no sir, three bags full, sir," Sylvia said, curtsying as she sidled around him to pull a small tray from the cupboard. "Whatever you say."

"What's gotten into you?" Greg wanted to know, giving her a suspicious glance. "Did Hazel read your fortune while you were down there?"

"Nope."

"There must be some reason for this sudden exuberance," Greg persisted.

Dany kept her attention on finishing the sandwiches as she listened to their casual exchange, often sounding more like a brother-sister relationship than anything else. On the other hand, that embrace she'd interrupted at the abandoned ranch wasn't particularly haphazard. Far from it. Which showed this was merely camouflage for the audience. She deposited the cut sandwiches on the plates with unnecessary force and wondered why she persisted in including a half-baked psychiatric analysis on the menu too.

The tail end of Sylvia's next comment brought her abruptly back to the present. " . . . so I just asked if she knew what time Evan and Jeff might get back tonight."

Greg paused in the midst of filling four coffee mugs. "But Evan told us he wasn't sure he'd get here. You were in the study when he mentioned it."

"Well, he apparently announced something else to Hazel, because she said that they'd definitely be back before nightfall." Sylvia came over to transfer a sandwich and bestow a dazzling smile on Dany. "That means I can go fishing."

"What in the dickens does my stepfather have to do with that?"

Sylvia put the sandwich plate on the tray with a flourish and reached for a mug of coffee to go alongside it. "Evan? Not a thing. Jeff invited me earlier. Apparently there's a big sturgeon down in the pool around the river bend that he's been trying to catch. You know that huge hook tied to the nylon rope down on the dock—well, that's what he uses."

Greg shoved his hands in his pockets and gave

her an indulgent smile as she hoisted the tray. "Be careful with that and don't waste any time coming back—otherwise you'll miss out on lunch."

"Aren't you the least bit excited about the fishing trip?"

"I wasn't invited," he pointed out good-naturedly. "Besides, I asked Jeff about fishing yesterday and he said you need a license."

"Not to watch," Sylvia said simply. She twirled the tray as she started down the hall. "I'll be back."

"It's too bad that you didn't plan ahead and buy a license," Dany said to Greg. "I wouldn't hold my breath waiting for a sturgeon dinner, but there's excellent trout fishing on the river."

"Maybe there'll be another time," Greg said, picking up his sandwich plate with one hand and his coffee with the other. "It's too cold to eat out on the deck, I suppose."

" 'Fraid so." She picked up the other sandwiches and trailed him to the table by the window, and then went back to get the two remaining mugs of coffee.

"Sorry." Greg stayed on his feet until she'd gotten seated, and then pulled up his chair. "I was thinking of something else."

"If it's about Sylvia going with Jeff—you don't have to worry. It's breezy on the river and that sturgeon has been hanging around waiting to be caught for years, so I doubt if Jeff will have any luck tonight."

Greg frowned and paused before taking a

swallow of coffee. "You're probably right, but I don't follow your reasoning."

Dany's color rose in her effort to spell it out. "I just meant that the fishing trip won't last long—if I know Jeff."

Greg's eyebrows went up as the light dawned. "Oh, that!"

"Yes, that," Dany said exasperatedly.

"Of course, it's possible that Jeff might have things on his mind other than that sturgeon—"

"Like what?" Sylvia wanted to know, coming up behind them.

"You'd better ask him the next time you see him," Greg said, getting to his feet, without any dismay at the interruption. "I'm not sure that he'd approve of my passing the news along at this point."

"You make it sound awfully mysterious," Sylvia complained as he helped her with her chair and sat down again.

"That's only because you have an overactive imagination." Greg took a bite of sandwich and made an approving noise in his throat. It was several seconds later before he remembered to ask, "What about Hazel?"

"She's still on top of her bed, but I noticed that she gave her sandwich an approving look."

"Then she can't be very sick," Dany said, amused. "We should have offered milk toast."

"Or gruel." Sylvia took a bite of sandwich, barely managing to mumble, "I've always wondered how you make gruel."

"If we have to exist from that refrigerator much longer, we may find out," Dany replied. "From the look of things, it's either going to be hash tonight or waffles. Thank heaven there are still plenty of potatoes and eggs."

Greg grinned and turned to Sylvia. "Why don't you tell Jeff to forget about that sturgeon and concentrate on trout instead? This is getting down to basic supply and demand."

"Maybe he'll bring back some more steaks. You both worry too much."

Greg raised an eyebrow, saying to Dany, "At least we know who to eliminate if it comes to push and shove."

"No work—no food," Sylvia told him cheerfully. "Any more coffee?"

"In the pot," Greg replied, and shook his head when she came back and waved it suggestively over his cup. "Not for me, thanks. I'm getting back to work and you'd better come as soon as you're finished. I'll be lucky to get any sense out of you the rest of the day."

Sylvia's expression turned thoughtful as she replaced the pot on the stove. "That reminds me, Dany. I must move my things from the bedroom into your cottage sometime this afternoon. I'd hate to have Evan think that I'm dragging my feet deliberately."

"Don't worry," Greg said as he got to his feet and put his empty plate by the sink. "I'll help you move the stuff. We can do it right now—or, at least, as soon as you finish lunch."

"That's too good an offer to miss," Sylvia mumbled, taking a hefty bite. "I'll be right there."

They watched him disappear into the master bedroom an instant later, and Sylvia tossed an apologetic smile in Dany's direction as she piled her empty plate on top of Greg's. "We're leaving you with the dishes again. I'd volunteer except that . . ."

"You have other things to do." Dany's glance was sympathetic. "I understand. You'd better get going—Greg doesn't wait around for long."

Dany tossed a mental coin after Sylvia left the kitchen, and her conscience triumphed. If she hurried in clearing the dishes, Hazel wasn't likely to appear. Besides, she wasn't anxious to get back to the task of sorting the remainder of her belongings. It was only the prospect of an exorbitant freight bill that had made her winnow the lot in the first place.

It didn't take long to restore the kitchen to an acceptable shape, but it was late afternoon when she finally finished going through the last box of her photographs and old correspondence. The sound of the door opening brought her head up and she blinked with surprise at seeing her stepfather's figure on the threshold.

"Oh, you're back," she said, getting to her feet and then grimacing. "Damn! My foot's asleep! I've been sitting on the floor too long."

"It looks as if you've made considerable progress," Evan said, his glance going swiftly over her belongings that she had stacked against the wall. "Are you taking most of this with you?"

"I planned on it." She matched his cool tone. "If it's all right with you."

"My dear girl—whatever would I do with your books and sentimental claptrap? Nostalgia isn't my line of country at all."

Dany shoved her hands in the pockets of her jeans and faced him defiantly. "You made that clear right after you persuaded my mother to marry you. I'm just glad that she never found out about some of your other quirks." Her lips curved slightly, but there wasn't any humor in her expression. "You were smart to keep those hidden."

A tinge of color swept up under her stepfather's cheekbones. "And you'd have been smarter if you'd tried to get along with the new order. You might have been included in the payoff then."

"No way. I don't care for your rules." Dany brushed her hair back from her face with a weary gesture. "None of it matters now. I'll be gone tomorrow and then we won't get in each other's way any longer."

He shrugged. "That's up to you. It won't matter, because I don't plan to stick around this place more than a day or two myself. The way things are going, my buyers should sign the earnest-money agreement tomorrow."

"Then your sale's going through?"

"Naturally." His tone was smug as he preened visibly. "And without any whopping commission to Fremont Consultants, either. I could have done the whole thing myself if I'd waited a little longer."

"You'll certainly have to pay Greg's travel expenses and some sort of a fee. From what I've seen in the past, a healthy one."

"That's nothing compared to the amount his company would charge if they handled the sale," Evan said with an airy wave of his hand. "Greg won't be happy but he'll learn that some of us amateurs know how to handle business matters, too."

"When it comes to handling money," Dany said dryly, "you were giving lessons in your cradle. Mother mentioned how 'efficient' you were in controlling her estate."

His color rose again under her accusing glance, but he wasn't visibly disconcerted. "Your mother was a trusting person. It was part of her appeal."

"Spare me the platitudes."

He shrugged again. "Only one person can be in charge handling finances. I tried to make that clear to her, but by then . . ."

" . . . She was too ill for anything to matter." Dany chewed on her lower lip, determined not to let him see how much his uncaring, often deliberately cruel behavior at the time still disgusted her. "There's no point in discussing it now. I could use a few more cartons to pack those books in," she said, changing the subject.

"Speak to Jeff about it. Or Hazel. They might be able to find some."

"Whatever you say." She glanced across at him

as a sudden thought struck her. "Have you told your housekeeper that she'll be out of work again?"

"My housekeeper?" He paused with the door halfway shut. "Oh, you mean Hazel." As he saw Dany's lips twitch with amusement, his bony chin asserted itself. "There won't be any trouble. She's an old acquaintance."

"How nice." Dany kept her tone carefully polite. "Do you think she'll be feeling well enough by now to tell me how to cook dinner?"

"I haven't any idea," Evan snapped. "That's between the two of you. I can't be bothered with such things."

"Obviously you haven't been eating many meals at home lately or you'd change your priorities."

"The only thing I'm interested in at this moment is one phone call. They're going to relay it to the forest service headquarters and I'm going downstream now to make sure that everything's arranged. I'll be back after dinner."

"But that's just a couple miles downriver," she said, puzzled. "It doesn't take any time for Jeff to make that run."

"Jeff won't even have to wait—he can come back and pick me up before it gets too dark," Evan announced as he stepped out onto the porch, lingering just long enough to add, "The new ranger at the station is from the Midwest and feeling a little homesick. When I told him Illinois was my old stamping ground, he was kind enough to invite me to dinner. Naturally that was before I knew that you all would be here. So if I don't see you tonight, I'll undoubtedly see you in the morning before you leave.''

His wintry smile seldom reached his eyes, and this time wasn't any exception, Dany thought. ''I'll look forward to it,'' she said, crossing her fingers behind her back. ''Enjoy your dinner.''

When he'd gone on his way, she sank onto the edge of a folding chair, completely unnerved by their encounter. Which was ridiculous, she told herself fiercely. The man didn't have any control over her now; she didn't even have an obligation to be pleasant as she had during those months when her mother was still alive. There was nothing that Evan could do any longer, and it suddenly felt wonderful to be free.

Hazel was still among the missing when she dropped in at the lodge later on to see if dinner was on anybody's agenda. A roar from the river drew her to the window and she looked down to see Jeff bringing the *Belle* back into the dock. On an impulse, she went out to the deck and called to him. ''Want to go for a walk?''

He looked up, obviously startled to see her. ''I thought you were busy with the packing bit,'' he called back.

''All finished.'' She spread her palms. ''Except for about two boxfuls. And first I have to find the boxes.''

''I can get those for you tomorrow,'' he said, starting up the path toward her. ''What about

Sylvia? I promised her a fishing trip if she can make time for it."

"That's right—I'd forgotten. I think she's still working, but I'll find out," Dany called, and went back to the lodge. After knocking on the study door, she opened it and stuck her head around the edge hesitantly. "I'm sorry to bother you," she said as Sylvia looked up from her calculator and Greg frowned behind the desk. "Jeff and I wondered how much longer you'd be. He's thinking of that fishing trip—actually there's not much time because he'll have to pick up Evan again before dark."

Greg sighed audibly and raked his fingers through his hair. "If I had a choice, I know what I'd do. Go on, Sylvia, you might as well salvage a part of the day."

Sylvia bounced to her feet, an unbelieving smile on her face. "Greg—do you mean it? I'm not finished with this . . ."

"I'll tell Evan that the final draft will have to be mailed to him. I'm a little tired of his orders today." He jerked a thumb toward the door. "Go ahead, before I change my mind. Do me a favor, though . . ."

Sylvia paused with one foot in the hallway and her eyes gleaming with excitement. "Just name it."

"Don't catch that damned sturgeon. Knowing you, we'd have to take it back downriver tomorrow and have it stuffed, and there simply won't be room in the boat."

"I'll make sure that Jeff never gets the bait on the hook," she promised, and disappeared before he could issue any more orders.

"If there's something I can do to help . . ." Dany offered halfheartedly, unsure of how to phrase it.

"Exactly what did you have in mind?" Greg asked, leaning back in the desk chair to survey her as she stayed by the door.

He was amused by her gesture—just as she'd feared—and it triggered an illogical anger in her breast. She snapped, "I didn't come here to play games—that's for sure. Taunting people may be fun for you, but right now I could do without it."

"Temper, temper," he reproved. "Is that just righteous indignation after a tiresome day, or are you sulking because Jeff invited Sylvia and neglected to ask you?"

"That's ridiculous. I told you that I was going for a walk, and since you obviously don't want me for anything—"

"Oh, I wouldn't say that," he cut in, his tone silky. "But I'm sure your offer didn't cover what I have in mind."

"It certainly didn't," she flashed back, annoyed because he'd no sooner sent Sylvia on her way before turning to a little idle flirtation just to keep his hand in. "And if that's all you can think about, maybe *you* should take a walk—or a cold shower."

"One thing sure—it would be a cold shower if I took it in this place." The front of his chair crashed down on the floor as he leaned over the desk again, clearly tired of the discussion. "And as long as you stay hovering by the door, you can't accuse me of laying a finger on you."

Her shoulders went back in a defiant gesture. "I'll go out into the hall. It's even harder that way."

He ignored that and bent over his papers again. "I'd limit that walk of yours if I were you. I imagine Hazel will be fixing dinner before long."

"Tell her not to bother so far as I'm concerned. After I get some fresh air, I'm going to bed early."

His head came up. "That's ridiculous. You have to eat."

"I'm not hungry."

He got to his feet then and walked slowly over to where she stood at the door. "Look, if it's something I've said—I'm sorry. I certainly don't mean to make you lose your appetite and force you to take to your bed."

"It isn't that." She decided to lay her cards on the table because it was tiresome clutching them close to her breast—especially when that concerned look on his face showed he was telling the truth. "I just had a final go-round with Evan and it left me in a nasty mood. I should apologize to you, really," she owned with a crooked smile. "You got the brunt of it."

"You had plenty of provocation." Greg shook his head ruefully. "There's something about you

—every time you come into range, I see a red flag and start pawing the ground."

Her smile broadened at the imaginary scene. "You haven't mentioned the steam coming from your nostrils. . . ."

"Not really. I just haven't gotten around to it yet." As he reached out, she took an instinctive step backward and found herself against the edge of the door. "You're doing it again," he said in a dangerously level tone.

"Doing what?" The words came out in a gulp.

"Cringing. That's waving a red flag in front of a man with a vengeance. I've often wondered if you do it deliberately," he continued as he pulled her close, "instead of batting your eyelashes or wearing a neckline down to your navel."

"You certainly can't accuse me of that," Dany said, finding herself muttering into a shirt front and vividly aware of his tanned chest just a whisper away.

"Hardly. You're so deep in gray flannel most of the time that I have to peer through the layers. Even now." His hand slid leisurely down the side of her quilted nylon jacket.

"That's because I'm going for a walk," she managed breathlessly, and tried to push away from his chest.

"In good time. It's taken me months to get this close, so I'd better take advantage of it before you haul off and . . ."

Dany never did find out what she was supposed

to haul off and do, because at that moment his lips came down and she forgot everything in the surprise of his sudden embrace. That first kiss was gentle as a butterfly's touch at the corner of her mouth, but then Greg groaned and tightened his clasp as his lips moved to cover hers. There wasn't any indecision about the second kiss; it was possessive and ruthless, so disconcerting that she parted her lips instinctively. Greg felt her relax against him as it deepened, and slid his arm down to her hips to pull her close against him.

When he finally let her come up for air, Dany found herself clinging to his shoulders for dear life so that she wouldn't collapse on the rug at his feet. Greg was breathing hard too, she noticed, but he put her firmly from him, even turning her toward the hall as if he didn't want her wasting any more of his time.

"Go take your walk," he told her brusquely. "You're a hell of a distraction. I'll see you when you get back."

It was difficult to make sense when her head was still whirling and her breath seemed stuck down at her ankles, but Dany tried. "I still don't want to make an appearance at dinner."

"That's all right." The words came over his shoulder as he turned back to the desk. "I'll probably knock on your cabin door later and check that you're okay. It's practically on my way."

She lingered on the threshold an instant longer,

strangely loath to leave. "On the way to what?"

His grin was fast and rueful as he sat down at the desk. "That cold shower I was talking about earlier. I have a feeling that by then I'll need it."

7

As a form of exercise, Dany's walk was of
dubious value. To tone the muscles, body-fitness
gurus advocate brisk strides and breathing
deeply; Dany found herself meandering along the
path and sitting on convenient flat rocks so that
she could stare at the rushing water of the Snake
below. When a squirrel moved onto the end of the
fallen log to inspect her quiet seated figure, she
gave him a half-smile, barely aware of his
presence.

It wasn't surprising, since those last minutes in
the study with Greg were the only things etched
vividly into her consciousness just then. It was
ridiculous to place any significance on two kisses
—"absolutely ridiculous," she said aloud, and
noticed that the squirrel decided to leave the
scene at that point. Apparently he didn't approve
of humans who went around talking to themselves, and she couldn't blame him.

Sometime soon she'd have to figure out what to
do with the rest of her life, but it was nice to relax

and not fight the currents for a few hours. At the moment, it was an unexpected bonus to have Greg's support in helping to cut her final ties with Evan and her old home. Once she'd managed that, she'd have to give serious thought to this new relationship with Greg—she couldn't bring herself to think of it as anything else. He might slide in and out of affairs with consummate ease, but she knew very well that she'd end up as an emotional basket case if she tried the same thing.

She drew a line in the dirt of the path with the edge of her shoe sole and surveyed it solemnly. Some people crossed over and still managed to function; it was a pity that she'd been brought up a different way.

She got to her feet in a determined movement that sent the squirrel scurrying from his observation post behind a dead tree stump. If she didn't get back down the path to the resort before dark, she'd be stuck until morning, and that wasn't to be considered. Her bed in the cottage might be below-standard, but compared to a dirt trail, it was the Ritz itself.

There was the sound of music coming from the lodge as she reached it some twenty minutes later, but she wasn't tempted to detour inside. A hot shower, taken before Evan and Hazel could switch off the generator, sounded much more appealing by then. There was a bar of chocolate which she'd providentially packed in her suitcase if hunger pangs became too strong to ignore. It was too bad that she hadn't known what a poor cook Hazel was, so she could have included some trail rations as well.

On her way to the bathhouse, she contemplated the possibility of Greg coming to call and then told herself not to let her imagination get out of hand. Probably by then, Evan had him securely anchored to the couch in the lodge, trying to find the best tax loopholes for his projected sale.

Dany did such a good job of convincing herself that when the knock came on her cottage door a half-hour later, after her shower, she looked up with surprise. "Who . . . who is it?" she managed to ask in an unsteady voice.

"Now, who were you expecting?" Greg's dispassionate reply made her suspect that his shower must have been cold indeed!

"Half a minute," she said, reaching for her wool robe, which she'd left on the end of the bed.

"Not much longer," he said through the door. "Evan and Hazel are about to go into their 'lights-out' routine."

"I'm coming," she replied breathlessly as she went over to pull it open. She swallowed to see him lounging against the porch post and wondered if she'd ever get over the way his presence took her breath away.

Such a malady wasn't bothering Greg. His quick glance over her was his usual comprehensive one and her floor-length navy-blue robe with striped pajama cuffs at the bottom clearly didn't impress him. At least not in the way Dany had hopefully fantasized.

"That looks almost as good as another blanket," he commented at the end of his survey. "You wouldn't like to part with it tonight, I suppose."

It wasn't an offer that merited a slap in the face, but Dany felt a tremendous urge to kick him in the shins. To think she'd been nervous about meeting him after that passionate interlude earlier.

"Not really," she managed, determined that she could match his manner, "unless you're prepared to match it with sables—and considering the temperature in here, there'd have to be a bundle of them. I'm sure that you didn't come just for moonlight requisitioning."

He appeared to consider and then chose his words carefully. "Not exactly. Although I could do worse," he said, running his glance over the robe again. "Actually this is sort of a . . . diplomatic mission."

She tightened her belt in absentminded fashion. "Curiouser and curiouser," she quoted. "You might do better with a different approach."

"Okay. But you can get the suspicious look off your face. This doesn't concern you. At least not directly."

"I still don't understand . . ."

"Look, you're a big girl now," he said, shoving his hands in his pockets. "You must have seen that Sylvia and Jeff have a thing going. I doubt if it's serious, but I don't like to interfere."

Dany bit her lip, torn between elation and a

strange desire to comfort his wounded feelings. "You won't have to worry in the long run. I've seen Jeff operate before. He's inclined to go off the deep end, but it never lasts."

"Even so, I'm not going to be the one to mention it to Sylvia. Not in the mood they're in tonight. I don't know what happened on that fishing trip, but . . ." He broke off, shaking his head.

"I still don't see what this has to do with me," Dany pointed out. Greg may have thought he was being diplomatic, but after all that had happened, he surely couldn't expect her to calm the waters of his relationship with Sylvia.

Greg looked embarrassed but he'd rubbed a hand over his face before Dany could make sure of his expression. "To put it delicately," he began, "the housing arrangements around here don't do much for romance. Since there are only two available cottages—"

"You mean that I'm in the way?" she asked incredulously as he paused again. When he didn't answer, she went on, "I really don't see what I can do to help in this case."

"Then you're not as bright as I thought you were. There are two beds in my cottage. You can start the night there and give them a clear field here. It needn't take long. Later on, I'll cruise around and see if you can move back."

"You mean, run a bed check?" she asked, as if she couldn't believe her ears.

"Not literally, for God's sake. They just want to have some time alone." He glanced at his watch. "Make up your mind—I told them that I'd speak to you."

By then Dany was so confused that she would probably have agreed to anything. She shook her head, wondering if it would help to go up and stick it under the cold-water faucet in the bathhouse. "I shouldn't have skipped dinner," she muttered.

"I don't know what that has to do with anything, but there's a flask of coffee at my place— for what it's worth. You'd better hurry, though, or you'll be drinking it by candlelight."

She looked around the room in dazed fashion. "I suppose I'd better get dressed again."

"There isn't time for that," Greg said with another glance at his watch. "You might drag along those blankets."

"Don't be silly," she said scornfully. "Even Romeo and Juliet would need some covers after ten minutes in this place."

"Not if you close the window—"

"It isn't open." She peered up at him, wondering if it were the pale overhead light that made him look tense. Probably this newest development with Sylvia was more disturbing than he was letting on. She reached for her jacket then and pulled it over her shoulders. "All right, I'm ready. Oh, damn!" The last came when the overhead bulb flickered out. "Where's my flashlight?"

"Here." There was a rustle before a metallic crash at floor level. "At least, it was here." Greg turned on his own flashlight and located the one he'd just knocked off the table. "I hope it still works."

"If it doesn't . . ."

"It does," he said, making sure before handing it to her. "No need to get upset."

"Of course not," she said, following him out onto the porch and closing the door behind them. "I'm crazy about these impromptu pajama parties. Why in the deuce couldn't you just tell Jeff to cool it until they're back in Lewiston?"

"Obviously you have no soul."

"It isn't Jeff's soul that I'm talking about," she complained, pulling up beside him on the porch of his cottage and waiting while he fumbled with the doorknob. An instant later, he stepped aside to wave her ahead of him. She surveyed the bleak room in the light of their two flashlight beams and said, "At least we won't be disturbed by editors from *House Beautiful* coming to call." Hearing a rustling behind her, she turned to see Greg opening his suitcase. "What are you doing now?"

"I don't plan to spend the rest of the night in these clothes. Although I don't know why I bother," he went on calmly. "This sport coat already looks as if I've slept in it. Even so, another eight hours won't help."

Dany opened her mouth to protest until the logic of his statement penetrated. She kept her glance on his side of the room until she saw him hauling out a pair of dark green pajamas and a matching lightweight travel robe.

He looked up then and his mouth quirked as he encountered her gaze. "I'd offer to change up in the bathhouse, but it's a hell of a lot easier here. If naked bodies offend you . . ."

The sagging springs on the bed made a pinging noise as she flounced onto it and turned her back.

"I was sure we could work it out," Greg continued.

There was a silence while Dany kept her attention on the chintz curtain with a missing hook which was drooping from the brass rod. She did her best to ignore the sounds at the other side of the room. "How long is all this going to take?" she asked finally. "Jeff and Sylvia's rendezvous, I mean."

He appeared to consider. "I suppose it could depend on the weather."

"That's a big help."

"Sorry, I never claimed to have all the answers." He came up beside her at the edge of the bed then, carrying a pillow.

She stared at it suspiciously as he put his flashlight on the windowsill to provide a kind of indirect lighting. "What's that for?"

He turned, frowning. "It's just the pillow from the other bed."

"I *know* that. What's it doing here?"

"Because this is where the blankets are," he explained patiently. "They're the things you're sitting on. And now, if you wouldn't mind moving over . . ." He barely waited for her to shift toward the end of the bed before pulling down the covers. "You may have a wool robe, but I don't, and that air feels like it's off McMurdo Sound," he added getting into bed.

"But I thought we were just going to wait until I could get back into my place," she protested, her voice rising. "I didn't know you were going to bed!"

"For my money, there's not much of a choice." His gesture encompassed the rest of the room. "Of course, if you have any suggestions . . ."

Dany looked around wildly, her glance going over the other bed, which showed only a lumpy mattress, before it came back to face him accusingly. "You've got all the covers."

"Two blankets. Two pillows."

"I'm entitled to half."

He patted the bed beside him as he said, "Be my guest. Normally bundling doesn't appeal to me, but I'm willing to make exceptions considering the temperature in here. Would you now kindly shut up and get under the blankets—you're creating a hell of a draft."

It certainly didn't sound like an offer for seduction, Dany thought, as she hovered undecided. Unless a man wore a size-two hat and a size-seventeen shirt, he'd know that the conditions didn't lend themselves to anything except survival, and from Greg's impatient look he wasn't in any doubt. It would take far more than a wool bathrobe and a pair of wrinkled striped pajamas to have any effect on him. Possibly Cleopatra and the Queen of Sheba rolled into one, she thought with inward amusement as she went around to the other side of the bed and got in beside him.

"Something's amusing you?"

There was a dangerous undertone to his voice which showed that he wasn't missing a thing, despite the room's dim lighting.

"I can't imagine what it would be," Dany retorted, getting her expression under control as she punched the extra pillow into position behind her back. Then she scowled at him as he shifted down on the mattress. "You're not going to sleep?"

He came up again on one elbow. "I thought that was the general idea of going to bed."

"Well, yes." She squirmed under his level gaze. "It is normally. But I thought you were going to stay awake so you could go back and check on my cottage."

"That's apt to be a while. Don't worry, I'll wake up. If you're worried about it, there's a travel alarm around here someplace. I think it's in the top of my suitcase," he added, settling down again and pulling the covers up over his shoulder as he turned his back to her.

The last maneuver yanked Dany's corner of the blankets from her shoulders to her waist. Two seconds later, she knew he was right. There was a hell of a draft! She considered getting up to find the travel alarm, but as soon as she left the bed, Greg would manage to pull the rest of the blankets into the cocoon he was fashioning with masculine thoroughness.

She bestowed a baleful look at his head on the pillow. It was a wasted one because his eyes were peacefully closed and from his relaxed breathing, it wouldn't be long before he was sound asleep. And to think she'd worried about propinquity!

Suddenly making up her mind, she slid down on the bed beside him and heaved what was left of the blankets onto her shoulder with a mighty tug —hoping that the maneuver might at least spark a feeble outburst. But as she lay motionless, only the sound of Greg's even breathing could be heard in the freezing room.

Probably she'd wake up in an hour or so herself, Dany thought dispiritedly as she reached to turn off the flashlight. Then she could send Greg on his rounds. In the meantime, it was foolish not to get some sleep herself. The warmth from Greg's long form beside her was certainly an improvement over her cold bed of the night before, so she might as well take advantage of it. Especially, she decided with some bitterness, since it was the only advantage anybody was going to take of anything. With that thoroughly muddled grammatical conclusion, she fell sound asleep herself.

It was the murmur of voices which disturbed her and, even then, the awakening was a gradual one. Dany first became aware of a feeling of warmth and well-being. That realization made her snuggle down and bury her nose contentedly into a convenient burrow—a burrow which accepted her overtures by holding her even tighter. She would have drifted contentedly off to sleep again if the nearby voices hadn't struck a discordant note in her dreams. It took a second or two for Dany to decide that those voices were familiar and still another interlude before a laughing comment of "Sylvia, honey, if you keep on distracting me, we never will get down to breakfast," made her eyelids flutter upward. They stayed open through Sylvia's giggle and breathless comment of "That's libel—who's distracting who? Besides, I thought you'd be sleeping in this morning."

"Not much chance of that," retorted Jeff's voice from outside the cottage window. "The *Belle* wasn't set up for overnight guests—that forward bunk is barely big enough for a box of groceries. I was awake an hour ago."

Dany felt an instant of sleepy remorse for him, thinking it was a pity he couldn't be as comfortable as she was right then, and snuggled into her pillow again, fully intending to go back to sleep.

It was only when the pillow responded, and she felt a weight slide down from her waist, that her head came up a cautious six inches. The sight of Greg sprawled beside her brought the memories surging over her like a torrent of white water.

Only those memories of the night before didn't bear any resemblance to the scene in front of her, she thought, trying to pull herself together. Then it had been all neat and tidy—with two people on two sides of the mattress. One thing stayed the same; Greg still had a lion's share of the covers, with the remainder on the floor beside him. It was the pale morning sunlight seeping around the edges of the curtains which had provided her toasty comfort, Dany decided, not knowing whether to laugh or cry. That and the fact that she'd used Greg's warm chest for a pillow. Apparently he'd cooperated wholeheartedly during the night; one arm was still draped over her hips and his head rested contentedly on their two feather pillows.

It took another breathless protest from outside to shift her attention from the man sleeping soundly at her side.

"Jeff, you idiot! Stop that!" Sylvia's protests weren't as forceful as they might have been, Dany felt. Even so, the role of unknown eavesdropper wasn't appealing. Under any other circumstances she would have dropped a shoe or something as a tactful suggestion that they move away from the cottage.

Dany considered possible alternatives and then realized that she wasn't in any position to make a grandiose gesture. First off, she certainly didn't want to advertise her presence in the wrong cottage and, after shooting a wary glance down at her sleeping bedmate, she didn't want to rouse *him* until she could safely make her escape.

Moments later she discovered that, other than

burying her head against Greg's shoulder, she couldn't help overhearing the rest of the confidences being exchanged outside. Jeff was saying to Sylvia, "Neither one of us would have to be up at this ungodly hour if we'd followed our natural inclinations. . . ."

"We went all through that," she protested. "I don't approve of sleeping around and I honestly am allergic to new paint."

"I can understand that." Jeff sounded resigned but tolerant. "But I know we surprised Evan and Hazel when you asked if you could roll out a sleeping bag in the storeroom to avoid the cottage paint job."

"And I saw Greg's eyebrows shoot up when you announced that you'd spend the night aboard the boat," Sylvia said with a low laugh. There was a pause before she added, "I'm sorry that you had such an uncomfortable time."

"There are ways you can make it better." Jeff's voice dropped to a deep tone that didn't need interpreting.

In the pause that followed, Dany drew in her breath, trying to cope with what she'd heard. And then she realized that Greg's broad chest, which brushed almost imperceptibly against her arm, had changed its rhythm. Her glance narrowed as she frowned down at him.

Greg's eyes came open to encounter her angry glance and then widened as she sat up abruptly.

"You'd *better* wake up," Dany said, her words colder than the temperature of the night before.

"Otherwise, you might never live to see another day. . . ."

Greg rose on an elbow and jerked his head toward the window, muttering, "Be quiet—they'll hear you."

"That'll be a switch, at least." Dany's glance remained scathing but her voice dropped as Jeff spoke again.

"I suppose we'd better break this up," he said regretfully to Sylvia. "Where are you headed now?"

"Back to the lodge, I imagine. It's a little early to break in on Dany just to pack this damp toothbrush."

Inside the cottage, Dany raised her eyes heavenward, giving thanks that some breaks were still coming her way.

"Well, in that case—you can put the coffee on. I still have to shave and shower, but it shouldn't take me long," Jeff replied.

"If you hurry, we might even be able to eat before Hazel and Evan surface," Sylvia replied, her voice fading somewhat as she evidently started down the path.

"Give me ten minutes—twelve at the most if there's any hot water," Jeff responded.

"Fair enough. I'll even pour your coffee."

Dany waited until their footsteps disappeared and she heard the slam of the bathhouse door. Then she slid her feet to the floor and turned to face Greg, cinching the belt of her robe tight with a motion that showed she'd like to be doing the same thing to his neck. "Of all the cheap, miserable, low, conniving tricks . . ." she began, and then broke off as he got out of bed beside her and stretched in languid fashion. "Obviously, you have all the morals of a tomcat, which is what I suspected from the beginning."

"It must be a great comfort to be right so often," he said, lifting her out of his way so he could pull the curtain aside and look out the window.

"Take your hands off me . . ." Dany broke off, noticing that apparently he was only too happy to do just that as he kept his attention on the scene outside. Sometime during the night, he'd shed his travel robe, and the top of his pajama coat was hanging open. Either the buttons had worked their way free or she'd managed to accomplish it when she'd been resting—no, nuzzling: she might as well call a spade a spade—on his chest earlier. Fortunately, she didn't have to worry about that, she thought, and sneaked a look downward at her own attire.

Greg caught her in the process of doing up the top two buttons when he turned back to face her. "Spare me the belated modesty bit," he ground out. "You'll leave in the same unblemished condition that you entered, so you don't have to suffer any traumas about it."

"That has nothing to do with the fact that you deliberately misled me," she flared back. "You knew very well that Sylvia and Jeff wouldn't be in the other cottage last night. I must have been the only person this side of Lewiston who didn't know about it."

"There was always a chance they could change their minds," he said with unconcern as he put on his robe and rummaged for his shaving kit in the suitcase.

"But you knew they wouldn't. . . ."

"So I knew it." He sounded heartily sick of the subject as he straightened to face her. "It seemed like a good idea at the time, and if you're sticking around waiting for me to grovel, you'll have a hell of a long wait." His glance went briefly to the window again. "Since you have a clear shot at getting back to your own roof undetected right now—I'd suggest you leave. Otherwise your friend Jeff will be hotfooting down the path and you'll have the name without the game. That's not nearly as much fun, believe me."

"Oh, I'll believe you, all right." The anger Dany had been trying to summon surged to the fore then, egged on by his caustic tone. "My God, you're the one who wrote the book. Well, I can tell you this—you can damn well finish this farce by yourself! I don't ever want to see you again once we get downriver today."

"Then you'd better have something to remind you of your mind-boggling experience," Greg snarled, pulling her roughly against him as she started for the door. "That way, it won't be a total loss for you, after all."

"Let go of me, you br—" Dany's furious exclamation was sliced off when his mouth possessed hers. She tried to escape but his hand was like steel at her back, unmoved by her ineffectual gyrations.

Then suddenly he pushed her aside and, as she reeled back breathlessly, saying, "Damn you, Greg Fremont! I hate you—do you hear?" he stormed from the room, slamming the door behind him.

It took another three or four minutes before she managed to get out of the room and make her way to her own cottage. It took almost as long then to find the doorknob and get safely inside, because of the flood of tears of fury and frustration that were streaming down her face.

8

By dint of some careful maneuvering, Dany managed later to get up to the bathhouse without encountering anyone on the way. She spent a long time under the shower, despite the cooling temperature of the water, hoping that she could camouflage her pink and swollen eyelids. Not for anything would she give Greg the satisfaction that he'd collected another name for his long list of victims. She made a vulgar splutter as she raised her face to the deluge of water. Some victim! The man hadn't done a thing to her all night long. He had good reason for his scorn, and the punishing kiss he'd bestowed at the last minute showed how she could have really had reason to complain.

The fact that he'd inveigled her to his cottage didn't even make him pause. Apparently the word "compromise" applied only to Victorian vocabularies and wasn't in his book at all.

Reaching that conclusion didn't improve

Dany's mood and she was thoroughly discouraged by the time she'd dried herself and dressed in the best emerald-green wool slacks and matching suede-trimmed jacket for the trip back to town. Even the perky red-and-green silk print blouse which normally raised her morale didn't help as she surveyed her reflection in the mirror.

Her frown deepened as she heard the roar of a jet boat's engines nearby. She made her way out to the path just in time to see the *Belle* negotiate the currents next to the resort dock and turn downstream. Her fleeting glance counted four people aboard, and it wasn't hard to identify Greg and Sylvia's figures seated at the stern.

Dany drew in a painful breath. She hadn't expected them to leave so soon, and certainly not to accompany Evan and Jeff. Her fear was confirmed when she went back to the cottage and found that Sylvia's belongings had been removed in the interval and were probably on board the *Belle.* Like a patient probing a throbbing tooth to make sure the hole was still there, she went on to Greg's cottage and found it vacant, with only the tumbled bed linen swept back to furnish any memories of the night.

She hadn't thought she could feel any worse, but as she went back out on the porch and contemplated endless years without seeing Greg again, she knew it was just the beginning of her misery. Living with wounded feminine pride was all very well but it made a poor bedfellow and the prospect prompted her to rest her forehead against the porch support and close her eyes in despair.

It was the sound of another jet boat—this one headed upriver—which made her straighten and start slowly down toward the lodge. She'd have to manage the transfer of her belongings somehow, and once she'd arranged for transport from Lewiston, she'd think about searching for another job.

Hazel met her as she went in the lodge. The housekeeper was shifting two suitcases from the hallway to a vacant spot by the front door when Dany crossed the threshold. "I wondered when you were finally going to show up," the older woman snapped. "Breakfast's over—unless you want to get yourself something. There's too much happening today for me to hang around the kitchen waiting for people to come to meals."

"I can manage easily, thanks," Dany said, trying to hide her dislike of the woman. She noted that the housekeeper certainly wasn't dressed for a day near the kitchen stove, arrayed in a striped blue-and-white suit that, while it didn't flatter her, at least was less flamboyant than her other outfits. The fuchsia sandals had been changed for high-heeled navy ones and she wore a pearl choker that, unfortunately, only emphasized her triple chin.

"There are still some things in the refrigerator that I haven't had time to clear," Hazel said, gesturing in that direction.

"Toast and juice will do fine," Dany assured her. Her nose twitched. "It smells as if there's another leaky heater in here."

Hazel eyed her with annoyance. "Some of us have more to do than stand around and complain all day. Besides, that heater is all the way down the hall, so the fumes can't bother you very much here. As I told Evan, I have no intention of freezing to death in this place before I get back to town."

Dany could have mentioned that she was more apt to die by asphyxiation if she kept on the way she was going, but decided it wasn't worth quarreling about. She didn't plan to stay around as an onlooker if she had any choice in the matter —a point that was necessary to determine right away. "I presume that Jeff will be back to take me downriver," she said as she opened a small can of tomato juice she'd found on the counter.

Hazel was headed back down the hall but she paused to shrug elaborately. "He'll be back—to pick up his things, if nothing else. You'll have to make your arrangements with him then. He simply issued his ultimatum this morning and then took off."

"I don't understand . . ."

"There's nothing complicated about it. It's just another case of an employee ignoring the loyalty due his employer. That young man certainly cut off any chance of severance pay, leaving without a proper notice like this."

"You mean Jeff's quitting?"

"Haven't I just said so?" Hazel patted her highly lacquered curls to make sure they were still firmly in place. "Evan might have let him stay on here until after the sale was completed, or even recommended him to the new owners, but not now."

"What's Jeff's going to do?"

"He didn't say. Just mentioned that he'd made other plans and Evan should hire another river pilot after today. Imagine!" She frowned as Dany disposed of the juice can and started toward the door again. "Is that the sum total of your breakfast? Honestly, you people! All Greg wanted was coffee this morning."

"Really?" Dany kept a noncommittal expression but she hoped desperately to learn if Greg and Sylvia were taking the first plane out or whether he'd made other plans.

"You'd think a man like that would have more sense," Hazel was going on, still affronted by her guests' eating habits. "I found him hard to understand all around." Her pale glance flicked over Dany's immobile figure. "Are you all packed?"

As Hazel's question registered, Dany threw in a mental towel. What difference did it make what anyone else was going to do? Her only concern was leaving White Water on the first boat. She faced the housekeeper squarely. "Almost— except for a box or two. I meant to ask earlier if I could have some. Evan said to check with you."

Hazel had opened her mouth to refuse, but Dany's last sentence made her reconsider grudgingly. "I don't really have enough to finish packing his things myself. Oh, well—I suppose you need them more, since you're leaving today. I can get one from my bedroom, and there's one that I just started to fill on the desk in Evan's study."

"I'll start with that," Dany said, moving toward the door. "I'm sorry to bother you with all this."

"Well, at least this confusion can't last forever," Hazel said, her high heels making an angry tattoo on the wooden floor as she went down the hall.

The box Hazel had mentioned was atop the desk and partially filled with her stepfather's belongings. Dany started lifting them out carefully, noting some old theatrical programs mixed with his business ledgers. It was surprising that he'd bothered with the old souvenirs, she thought, piling the papers onto the corner of the desk so she could completely empty the box. Once she'd finished and started to lift it off, she dislodged part of the stack. Muttering under her breath, she stooped to pick up the fallen papers and then stayed bent over the desk as a photograph from one of the old theatrical accounts caught her attention. Her glance flicked from the figure scantily attired in feather boas to the caption, and her eyes grew large as she read the faded headline and then the smaller print:

DANCER CHOOSES MARRIAGE OVER CAREER
Popular chorus graduate Hazel Lowery yester-

day revealed her recent marriage to Evan Monroe was responsible for her announced withdrawal from the musical production *Who's in the Bedroom?* scheduled to open at the Lyceum later this month. . . .

The sound that brought Dany's head up from the paper came from the hallway, and she saw Hazel standing in the doorway with an empty corrugated box at her feet. It was the sheer malevolence in the housekeeper's stare that kept Dany frozen beside the desk—the paper still clutched in her fingers.

If Hazel had sounded unfriendly before, it was nothing to the vitriol in her words as she spat them out then. "I told Evan it was a mistake to let you come back. He should have known that you'd be snooping around." The woman's thin lips were an ominous line as she surveyed Dany. "As long as you've dug out what you were looking for, you might as well stay in there and finish your reading."

The words barely left her mouth before she slammed the study door shut and, an instant later, Dany heard her turn the key in the lock.

Suddenly coming alive, Dany flew over to try the knob and then pounded angrily on the thick door. "Hazel, don't be ridiculous! Let me out of here! What do you think you're doing?"

"Making the best of a bad situation." The housekeeper's voice came clearly through the floor vent which opened onto the hallway. "I may have to change our plans, but that's nothing compared to what you'll have to do." The last words came with some effort, and there was a metallic thud to punctuate them. "I was going to throw this heater out, since you all complained so much," Hazel continued, "but it will do nicely for what I have in mind."

Dany stood frowning by the door, wondering if the woman had gone completely off her rocker. She was even more aghast when she heard Hazel's receding footsteps and then a slam from the outer door of the lodge.

The noise of the jeep starting was the final blow and Dany's cheeks paled. Surely the woman wasn't going to leave her locked in—it didn't make any sense. No sense at all.

It wasn't until she recognized the strong sickly fumes of the leaky gas heater curling up from the floor vent that Hazel's scheme all became clear.

Evan's former wife hadn't merely imprisoned and deserted her—she was doing her damn well best to kill her in the process!

9

Dany's innate common sense saved her at that point. Instead of being overwhelmed by her circumstances, she felt a surge of outrage at Hazel's diabolical action. Her first reaction was to sweep a blanket from the bed, stuffing it as firmly over the vent as possible, to at least slow those nauseating fumes. She swallowed then, determined not to think about her queasy stomach and the headache that was already starting to pound in her temples. A quick glance around the room convinced her that the most practical way of escape was the window that Evan had boarded up the season before. The planks were well-fitting and sturdy, but that didn't mean that she couldn't pry them off if she could find something to use as a wedge.

Evan's desk drawer didn't offer anything more serviceable than a ruler, and it took her only thirty seconds to break that and discard the remnants in disgust. She rubbed her fingers over her smarting eyes as she searched desperately around the room again, drawing a quick exasperated breath when she saw what she should have used at the beginning—the brass fireplace tools at the end of the hearth.

It was harder to ignore the spreading fumes by then, and there was a grim look on her face as she snatched up the poker and went to the window. Probably the best place to approach it was the top, she decided, and managed to pull the desk chair over to stand on. As she clambered up, she braced herself with one hand and used the poker to pry desperately at the edge of the board. At first she just gouged the wood, but five minutes later she'd loosened one nail. By then it was an effort to keep her balance on the chair, and she realized that she'd have to redouble her efforts or she'd never make it.

Just one plank off, she told herself, and she could smash the window glass underneath to let in that sweet freezing fresh air. She rubbed her face, trying to clear her vision, and then stabbed and pounded with the poker again—oblivious of everything but the splintered timber.

There was no warning when the door opened behind her, and she only caught a glimpse of a shadowy figure on the threshold as she sagged against the wall, barely aware of Greg's voice saying, "My God! What's going on in here?" Then, before she could say anything, he shouted over his shoulder, "Jeff, turn off that damned heater," and muttered an extremely profane comment as he scooped Dany into his arms to get her out of the room.

He dumped her into a chair on the deck a minute later, saying roughly, "That settles it—you're not going to be left alone again. You could have been killed in there. Who in the hell locked the door? And where's Hazel?"

"Gone in the jeep, I suspect," Sylvia answered hurriedly, bringing a damp washcloth out on the deck and offering it to Dany. "Maybe this will help."

"Oh, thanks." The cold water was wonderful on her hot face, and when Dany finally handed it back, she smiled gratefully at both of them. "I never thought it could feel so good to get out of a room." She glanced around as another thought struck her. "Where's Evan? Did he come back with you, too?"

"No way," Greg said. "We dropped him off at the forest service headquarters. He'd arranged to hitch a ride on another jet boat to get down to Lewiston this morning for his meeting to sign the sales agreement."

"But you planned to come back here all along?" Dany murmured, thinking of her needless despair.

"Naturally. How in the devil did you get stuck in that room in the first place?" Greg asked, staying stubbornly with his subject.

"Hazel." Dany raised her hands in a helpless

gesture. "She locked the door before she drove off."

"Just because you missed breakfast?" Jeff asked, coming out to join them.

"That isn't funny," Sylvia said, rounding on him.

"I didn't mean it to be. She'd need a reason for locking the door and leaving that leaky heater in the hall—unless she didn't know you were in there in the first place." He shot a thoughtful look at Dany.

"Oh, she knew. And I brought it on myself—only I didn't expect such a reaction." Seeing their puzzled faces, she got up, thankful that her legs were functioning properly again. "Wait here—I'll show you what I mean."

"Are you sure you feel up to—?"

"I'm fine." She cut into Greg's worried caution with a smile. "Just be sure to come after me if I'm not back in sixty seconds."

"Better still, I'll come along."

"We all will," Sylvia said, bringing up the rear with Jeff. "This I have to see."

The curiosity on their faces was replaced by stunned amazement when Dany exhibited the yellowed paper with the marriage announcement.

Greg didn't let her linger in the study but shepherded her back to the deck while they pored over the words again.

"I still don't see why Hazel would get so upset. At least, not enough to go locking people up and then taking off in that jeep," Jeff said, his good-looking features twisted in a frown. "Boy, will she regret it! That road's in terrible shape for the first ten miles. There's a washout that curls your hair."

Dany nodded, her own attention on Greg as he stared speculatively at the paper. She wasn't really surprised when he said, "I know of a reason to account for it, but it's so crazy . . ." Seeing Dany's intent look and then her slight nod, he turned to Jeff, announcing, "There's only one way to find out. Go down and get the *Belle* ready, will you? We're making a fast trip downriver."

Jeff blinked, obviously puzzled by the order. "All the way to the Bend?"

"Not right away. I want to use that phone at the forest service headquarters first off. Evan and Hazel needn't think they're going to get away with this," he said, his jaw stern and unforgiving.

"Are we all going?" Sylvia wanted to know.

"If you can be ready in the next two minutes . . ."

"I'm ready now," she said, hurrying down the path after Jeff before he could change his mind.

"Maybe you'd rather have her stay here with you," Greg said, frowning as he turned to Dany. "I don't want you here alone if Hazel should change her mind and double back."

Dany shuddered visibly. "That makes two of us, so I'm coming with you. And if you try to get away without me, I'll throw myself off the dock again—just to keep in practice."

"You needn't get the idea that you're going to win all the arguments from here on in," Greg protested beside her as they walked around the deck to the path. "Although I might let you get a word in on our anniversary."

Dany stopped in the middle of the path to stare up at him, wondering if she'd lost her hearing after all that pounding with the poker. "On our what?"

"You heard me."

He tried to urge her on again, but she shook off his hand at her waist. "Oh, no—you'll have to do better than that."

He shot a look at his watch and then softened as he saw her entreating glance. "I can do better later on when we've more time," he told her gently.

"It needn't take long."

"All right, then." He went on in a deep voice that wasn't completely steady, "I decided we might try sharing a bed again. Last night was pretty damned good—and it'll be even better when you're awake. We'll apply for a marriage license when we get back to Lewiston later today, and let's not have any arguments about it."

Dany drew an ecstatic breath, making no attempt to wipe away the tears that flooded her gaze.

Greg paused, feeling as if he could drown in those gorgeous blue eyes. "I can't remember when I didn't love you," he confessed. "And when I heard from your stepfather, I knew I had a perfect excuse to get to know you better. That's why I took his job in the first place, and I brought Sylvia along to see if I could make you jealous—anything to break through that wall of ice you'd erected in the office."

"When I think of that tall tale you concocted . . ." She shook her head reprovingly. "And you did a pretty good job of melting that wall yesterday."

"I'll do a hell of a lot better when I can put my mind to it," he promised, and grinned as Jeff gave a blast of the whistle from the *Belle*. "Let's call in the cavalry, my love, and put the villains on the run," he said, giving her a light but possessive kiss. "We still have plenty of work to finish."

She squandered another instant for the pleasure of drawing her finger along his cheekbone. "Before the sun sinks slowly in the west?"

He nodded, his glance so ardent that she trembled in his clasp. "Roll on, sunset," he said deeply, and took his time as he kissed her again.

It was a very nice sunset indeed five days later when darkness finally crept over the evergreen-covered hills surrounding Lake Coeur d'Alene in northern Idaho. Unfortunately, Greg and Dany, who were comfortably ensconced in the latest-model houseboat moored at a secluded spot along the shore, were paying little attention to the clear blue water in front of them or the attractive hotels of the resort town located just a few miles away.

"I suppose we really should get organized to go out to dinner," Dany said, trying to sound practical as she looked down at Greg, who was stretched out on the divan with his head in her lap.

"Mmmm. We could think about it first," he said, settling even more comfortably. "There's no point in making rash decisions and then regretting them later."

Dany burst out laughing. "We've been meaning to have dinner at that hotel ever since we arrived and we haven't made it yet."

"Henpecked already," Greg sighed, pushing up to sit beside her. "That's what happens as soon as a man gets married. Lord knows, I knew what was in store, but I still fell into the trap."

"You must admit that I've tried to treat you nicely since you took the fatal step." Dany's voice was soft as she reached over to smooth his forehead with her lips.

"Very nice," Greg said, managing to keep a solemn expression. "I always suspected you were a fast learner."

"Especially with such expert instruction," she agreed before pinching him hard on the ear.

"Ouch!" Greg pulled her across his lap and held her there. "Any more of that, madam, and there'll be serious retribution. Now that I've got my strength back . . ."

" . . . I'm quaking in my shoes. Or I would be," she said thoughtfully, "if I had any shoes on. I was afraid that you'd get back to normal fast."

His arm pulled her closer. "Mmmm—you said it. And it's only fair to warn you, Mrs. Fremont, that I expect to be in this frame of mind for the next fifty years or so."

"That's what I'm counting on," she assured him just as solemnly. "And it will be easier for you to concentrate, since you're finished dealing with Evan. Now what are you laughing about?"

Greg sat up straighter, his shoulders shaking. "If you could have seen his face when we showed him that printed account of his marriage to Hazel. Even then, he tried to bluster his way out until the police announced they had her in custody and that she'd confessed to everybody in the county that she'd never gotten a divorce. It's the first time I ever saw Evan completely at a loss for words."

Dany's lips quirked wryly. "I can imagine. Just think how he must have felt when Hazel appeared at White Water and demanded to be cut in on the goodies for her silence over the years."

"It certainly explains why he put the property on the market in such a hurry." Greg's expression became serious suddenly. "The frightening thing is, he came damn close to getting away with it."

"But surely his sale won't go through . . ."

"Darling, of course not." He gave her a quick hug. "The man was never legally married to your mother, so naturally the bequest in her will is null and void. We've never gotten around to discussing it, have we? I mean, what you want to do with White Water now that it's back in your family."

"Well, if you think it's a good idea"—she threaded her fingers through his as she spoke— "I'd like to donate some of the grazing land to enlarge the National Recreation tract which joins it on the south. And then I thought we might let Jeff run the lodge next season, since he wants to. I'm so glad about him . . ." she went on with a rush. "Imagine letting Evan blackmail him all this time just because he learned that Jeff was fool enough to get involved with those stolen Indian pictographs."

"But now that Jeff has confessed his part to the authorities and they've recovered the pictographs from where those dumb college kids buried them . . ."

"Jeff can go on with his life." Dany's glance was warm. "It's nice that Sylvia is backing him up all the way."

"After she tore a strip off him for getting involved in shady company." Greg sighed. "She's already told me that she wants a month off at the beginning of the season to help Jeff with running the resort."

Dany drew in her breath with surprise. "That's wonderful! Darling, do you think they might make a go of it?"

"I never give advice to women," he began, and then winced as his wife poked him in the ribs. "Well, you must admit," he went on after he'd chastised her properly, "I wasn't doing very well getting you to cooperate until we got to the canyon."

"Only because I thought you wanted me to provide a little dalliance whenever you could fit me into your schedule."

"Never has a man been so misunderstood." Greg tried to keep his mouth stern. "All along, my motives were beyond reproach."

"With just a few exceptions." She counted on her fingers to tick them off. "One proposition at Big Sky, a couple more at White Water, and then taking things into your own hands by shanghaiing me to the cottage overnight."

A look of satisfaction came over her husband's face. "And that did it!"

"Whatever are you talking about?" Dany asked, her tone not as steady as it might have been, as she felt his lightly exploring fingers.

"Taking things into my own hands. I was getting desperate by then, so I had to stoop a little . . ."

"You lied in your teeth," she told him severely.

"It's a damn good thing. Besides, I paid for it later that night. You slept right through, but I was awake for most of it—freezing to death . . . and wishing I could give in to my baser instincts. Fortunately"—there was a gleam of devilment in his eyes as he pushed aside a fragile panel of ivory lace that was the only thing separating them— "now I can."

Dany thought for an instant about trying to remonstrate with such a shameful philosophy, but when he pulled her close and started kissing her, everything left her mind except the sheer joy of being held in Greg's arms and knowing it was for a lifetime.

"Sweet, sweet, Dany. I didn't think it was possible to love a woman so much," he murmured against her satin skin. "Dearest, you don't really want to go out to that hotel for dinner, do you?"

When she merely reached over to nestle closer, he groaned with satisfaction. "I knew it! Who wants to eat out when there's such a feast at home? Now, for an appetizer . . ."

About the Author

Glenna Finley is a native of Washington State. She earned her degree from Stanford University in Russian Studies and in Speech and Dramatic Arts, with emphasis on radio.

After a stint in radio and publicity work in Seattle, she went to New York City to work for NBC as a producer in its international division. In addition, she worked with the "March of Time" and *Life* magazine.

As a producer, she had her own show about activities in Manhattan, a show that was broadcast to England. The programs were similar to those of the "Voice of America."

Though her life in New York was exciting, she eventually returned to the Northwest where she married. Currently residing in Seattle with her husband, Donald Witte, and their son, she loves to travel, and draws heavily on her travels and experiences for the novels that have been published. Her books for NAL have sold several million copies.